TINY

A catalogue record for this book is available from the National Library of Australia

ISBN 978-1-7643953-2-8 (Print)
ISBN 978-1-7643953-3-5 (eBook)

TINY

TREVOR L EVANS

TINY (Sergeant Ronald Harrison) is a young man who lives in a small regional country town, he goes to join the Police Force in the big smoke, where he works his way up to the rank of Sergeant, but he misses his small country town.

Tiny sees on the internet that they are looking for a Sergeant in his country town. He applies for the position and is accepted.

But, a country town is a little bit different to a big city, there is a fine line between friendship, and your duties as a Police officer, though you may have grown up with the people in this town, and know some of them very well, you must be able to establish your authority. Your heart is with the people, and you want to be with them, and protect them.

My name is Trevor; this story is completely my imagination. The characters I use, I have the deepest respect for, and do not want to offend in any way.

CHAPTER 1

I WAS FOLLOWING and early model Holden station wagon down the main street of my country town; I observed that there was something wrong with the way the car was moving, I couldn't pull the car over as there was too much heavy transport and other vehicles on the road, so I followed the car to the next set of traffic lights, the car turned left, and I pulled up alongside the car at the next set of traffic lights, I waved it over to the side of the road. The car pulled over to the curb, and I pulled up behind it. I put on my hat and started to get out of my car. (Tiny was one of those men who, when they get out of a car, seem to just keep on coming. He was 195 centimetres tall, and with his hat on, he looked even taller.) I went up to the driver's side door, and a young lady wound her window down.

'Good morning, Madam, may I see your driver's licence please.'

As she was looking in her bag, I noticed a young boy sitting in the front passenger seat; he looked about nine years of age, there was a young girl in the back seat, she looked about seven years of age, there was also a young baby about three months of age in a baby capsule. I noticed that there were blankets, some folded-up clothes on both sides of the children. I stepped back a couple of paces so that I could see inside the vehicle, where I saw two suitcases and other clothing. I went back to the driver's side window; the young lady handed me her driver's licence. I glanced at it, everything appeared to be in order, as I handed her back her licence I observed that she didn't appear to have been drinking, but her eyes looked very tired and weary, and she appeared to be holding back tears, I thought, taking my time, that she wasn't on drugs. 'Have you been sleeping in this car?'

'Yes, we have.'

'For how long?'

'This will be our sixth week.'

I hated asking the next question. 'Why are you sleeping in the car?'

'The man I was living with hasn't paid the rent in quite a while, and he just disappeared. I couldn't pay, I don't have any money, so I was evicted.'

I studied them all again. The children appeared to be well looked after; they were clean and tidy. 'Young lady, would you please follow me in your car? I will try to sort out your problem.'

She followed me up a side street and turned into another street. I pulled into a parking spot; she did the same. I asked her to follow me with the children, we went into a community building, I held open the glass door for her and the children.

The receptionist looked up, and in a warm polite voice asked, 'Good morning Tiny, how can I help you?'

I said, 'Good morning, Helen, is Joyce in?'

'Yes, but she's going to a meeting.'

I winked at her. 'I can never quite understand how everybody is going to a meeting and never coming back. I pushed open another glass door and asked the young lady to go through with her children. They walked down a corridor, opened another glass door, and I ushered the lady and her children through.

'Good morning, Joyce, are you having a lovely day?'

A lady slowly turned around on her swivel chair. 'No, Tiny, I have a meeting with the town bureaucrats, what do you want?' Her eyes saw the children, softened, then became serious again.

In a commanding voice, I spoke to Joyce. 'This lady and her children have been sleeping in their car for the last six weeks, they need a roof over their heads.'

Joyce looked at me, she was thinking to herself, If I argue with him, I won't win!

She said to me, 'You are a bloody headache,' but she grinned. 'You owe me another one, Tiny.'

She spun around to her desk, opened a drawer, and tossed some keys to me, which I caught with one hand. Joyce put a folder on the desk. 'Tiny, you're the sergeant; you do the paperwork. Now, if you will please excuse me, I have a meeting to go to.' She picked up her bag, walked over to the young lady holding her baby. 'She's absolutely beautiful, isn't she, I will enjoy watching her put Tiny around her little finger.' She walked out of the door, as she walked through the door, she put her hand behind her back and gave me a small gesture, and she was gone.

I sat down at her desk and filled out the paperwork, asked the young lady to sign the paperwork, then asked the young boy to come over and sign as well. I wrote down the address of the new lodgings on a piece of paper.

'Now, young man, your mother and I will go into the shopping centre to do some shopping. There is a playground outside where you and your sister can play.

I looked at the young lady. 'On this paperwork it states that you have a three-bedroom house, which will be fully furnished, it doesn't mention a TV, so now we have to go shopping. Do you have enough money?' She looked embarrassed.

'Not really Tiny.'

I thought, here we go again, and took out my wallet, and gave her $250. I asked her to get a receipt for everything she bought.'

The children enjoyed playing in the playground, and I enjoyed watching them. Their mother returned with the shopping trolley. I said to the young boy, 'You, young man, you can come with me in the Police Car,' and I put my hat on the boy.

Soon we arrived at their new house. I opened the front door and walked in; the house smelt new and fresh. The children ran in, exploring the house. I helped with the shopping and took the receipts. 'Now, I will leave it to you, and go and find a TV.' The young lady replied, 'I have a TV in the back of the car.'

'Good, that solves a problem. I hope you have a good night's sleep. Here is my card; if you have any problems, please feel free to phone me.'

I called the control room. 'On my way back.'

A female voice answered, 'It's your shout for coffee, and Chris O'Hara suggested jam doughnuts.'

I answered, 'Does he want the jam or the doughnut?' The remainder of my day was spent filling in all the paperwork.

When I got back home, my dog, Jack, was there to meet me. I gave him a big cuddle. 'You're a good dog, Jack, and you're my best friend, apart from Joyce, of course.'

The next morning, I returned to my desk and started to work on the roster for the next coming week. I am a very deep thinker and look at all the angles. Chris O'Hara put a hand on my shoulder and said, 'Good morning Tiny, Constable Terry's baby is due about now, if we put him on the front desk, he could get home easily when his wife goes into labour.'

'Yes, Chris, I agree with that.'

'Now Tiny, what have you been up to? Bending the rules a bit too far again?'

'Get to the point Chris, I'm extremely busy.'

'Well, all this paperwork has arrived for you, and they want you in Melbourne at 10.30 am tomorrow morning, in the Commissioner's Office. I will now leave all this paperwork with you, and I think you're going to be a lot busier.' He started to leave.

I grinned, 'Chris, it's your shout this morning, and I'll have a bacon and egg roll with my coffee.'

Chris waved his hand in front of his face and said, 'Anything great one, ask and you will receive.' He bowed his head and left.

I started to read through the paperwork. I had an appointment with the Commissioner at 10.30 am. I was to wear a business suit and bring a change of clothing for four days, my passport, and any other important documents. I would need another suitcase with all my Masonic regalia and a dinner suit. I read through it all again and thought; ours is not to wonder why, just do it and obey. I went through the rest of the paperwork and filled out a report concerning the lady from the previous day. Everything must be recorded.

Chris turned up with his coffee and an egg and bacon roll. I looked seriously at him. 'Chris, I would suggest that Margaret Percy drive me to Melbourne in the stations car, and then return here, that way you would still have the vehicle here, if we left it in Melbourne, with their budget cuts, we may not get it back! So if Margaret could pick me up at home at 6 am tomorrow, that would be great.'

Chris put his thumb up in the air. 'Consider it done.'

I drank my coffee and enjoyed my egg and bacon roll. Jess, who was running the front desk, put her head in the door. 'They're having trouble in the Top Pub again.'

'Thanks Jess, I'll sort it out, get Frank to meet me there.'

CHAPTER 2

I PICKED UP my hat and was on my way. I met Frank at the Top Pub in town. Two people walked out of the front door and said to me. 'We just came here for a quiet lunch, and we have to put up with that lot. They walked off, very annoyed. Frank and I walked up to the bar and said to the barman. 'Same problem?'

'Yes Tiny, same people, same young blokes turned up.'

Frank is a big, solid man with piercing eyes; you don't mess with him. He walked up to the young men, looking at them all, one hand up and started punching the palm of his hand with the other hand. 'I think you've all had enough to drink for one day, haven't you?'

They all glanced at him, then turned around and started to leave, quite quickly. I pointed to one of the young men; he was in his 20s. 'Not you, stay. Sit down.' I stood over him. 'This has to stop, you've been before the Magistrate three times, go before him again for disturbing the peace and you'll be locked up. I do not want you to disgrace your father, he was one of the best Policemen we had, and in performing his duty he became paralysed, now, we will go and see him, and see if we can sort this out. Get in my car.' I glanced at Frank; he knew exactly how to write out the report.

When we arrived at the young man's home, we walked in through the front door. I said to his mother 'Hello Dorothy.'

She looked at her son, 'Are you in trouble again? Your father is sick enough without you causing problems.'

We walked into the lounge, and I walked up to a man in a special wheelchair. 'Hello Michael,' the man never moved his head, only his eyes. 'Michael, we have to sort out the problem with your son. Do you remember George Sharmon?'

The man's eyes moved again. 'Well, now he's managing a cattle station up north. Would you like me to ring him and see if we can get this young man a job up there?'

The man's eyes moved again, letting me know he understood.

I took out his mobile phone and rang the number; I waited for three rings.

'Hello George, it's Tiny here. How are you doing up there, bit bloody hot down here. Do you remember Michael?

'Yes,'

'He was one of yours; would you have any work up there? His son needs to get away,'

'I had four people coming up from Melbourne to Brisbane, and one has had to pull out, so there will be a free seat on the plane,'

'Could you e-mail all that to me at home? Yes, my personal computer. Alright, I'll have him on his way in the morning. He's 20 years old. Michael is doing alright at the moment; he's still the same as you remember him. I'll tell him that. Thank you, George.'

'George said any day he can help, just let him know. Now, young man, be at your front door at 6 am. Don't even think about letting me down. Your schooling starts now.'

Dorothy started to cry; I put my arms around her. 'Yes, Dorothy, I understand. We are part of a big family. You can call us anytime you need us.'

I turned around and looked into Michael's eyes; I could see the tears starting. 'Catch up with you shortly, Michael.'

He turned to the young man. '6 am!' He nodded to them all and went back out to his vehicle. I sat there for a few minutes getting my mind together. There was a call on his radio. 'Yes, Tiny here'

'We have had a call from the young lady you helped yesterday; could you go and see her?'

CHAPTER 3

'Yes, I'm on my way.'

I knocked on the door, and the young boy opened it. A voice in the background said, 'I told you not to answer to anyone at the door.'

I thought it sounded like a man's voice. I put my hands on the boy's shoulder and stepped in. I saw a man there. 'Thought we had got rid of you.'

The young lady said, 'This is the man I was living with. He wants my half of the welfare money and my car.'

'Does he now? Wait here for a moment.' I went back out to my car and called on the radio. 'Tiny here, do we have anything on Sleazy?'

'Not at the moment, but Freddy's looking for him; he apparently owes Freddy money for his drugs.'

'Thank you, I'll call you back shortly.'

I went back into the house. 'Sleazy, Freddy's looking for you, he's got all his boys looking for you. I snatched Sleazy's wallet from his pocket and opened it. 'You've got a nice bit of money here, haven't you?'

Sleazy looked scared. 'You're not gonna give me over to Freddy, are you?'

'No, I don't like what he would do to you. Fishing bodies out of the river is not my thing.' I took $250 out of my wallet that will cover my expenses, then another $200, which I handed to the young lady, that should cover your expenses. Now I will take you down to the railway station, get on the train and go to Sydney. Freddy doesn't have jurisdiction there; it's not his patch. Let's go.

That's good timing; there's a train there. Get out and run.' Sleazy ran to the train and got on. I got out of my car and spoke to the stationmaster and sorted out his ticket. I watched the train pull out of the station. Now, the only thing I have to do is tidy up my papers and desk…

CHAPTER 4

I WAS PICKED up on time at 6 am. I put my suitcases in the boot with my man bag. 'Good morning, Margaret.'

She replied. 'Good morning, sir.'

I gave her the address to pick up the young man. 'Drop me off first, then drop the young man at the airport, escort him to the plane and make sure he gets on it.'

We didn't talk much police business; there wasn't any mention of things in front of the boy. We made good time getting to the big smoke. I got out of the car, got my suitcase and man bag out of the back. 'See you in a week or two, Margaret.'

I went up the steps into the foyer. 'Good morning, I'm Sergeant Harrison. I have an appointment with the Commissioner.'

'Yes, Sergeant Harrison, if you'd like to leave your suitcase with me, you are a little bit early. I suggest you go through that door there and have a coffee; they also do a big breakfast.'

'Thank you, that is a good suggestion.'

I sat down and had coffee and breakfast. I looked at it for a while and pondered to myself. Should I take a photo and send it to Chris? No, I wouldn't be able to see the look on his face. With a bit bigger tummy, I walked back out into the foyer, a gentleman told me where to go, a voice behind me said, 'Hello Tiny, we are both going to the same place.' I looked at him surprised, he was the Grand Secretary of the Lodge.

I said, 'Are we both in trouble, or is it just me?'

'Yes Tiny, I think we're both in trouble, but I must admit I'm concerned about you. Follow me Tiny to the chopping block.'

We both walked through a door that said Commissioner of Police. I swallowed to ease the pressure in this throat. The Receptionist said, 'If you would like to go through Sir, He is waiting for you.'

We both walked through the door. A man's voice called out 'Come in, come in' He got up from his desk and shook their hands. 'As you know gentlemen, I am Peter Smith, Commissioner of Police, the other man here is from ASIO,' we all shook hands, 'I think it's wise you do not know who I am, but please sit down, gentlemen.'

Peter Smith gestured to the man from ASIO to continue.

'Sergeant Harrison, may I call you Tiny?'

'Yes.'

'I can see why they call you Tiny,' he smiled. 'Now to business, you are here Tiny because we believe you're one of the few men who can solve big problems for us, and it's the way you work, you are a very experienced police officer, and very tactful the way you work and solve problems, your credibility is beyond reproach, why they let you go to a country town, I will not understand, yes, you do bend the rules, but you don't break them. So, we have a problem, there is a gentleman who works in higher places, we know he is an Australian, they call him Mr Dude, how he travels from one country to another so quickly, we're not sure, we've checked here and there are no learjets registered in his name, to him, he is a go between for selling arms and drugs, ivory and any other thing on the market that is controversial to the interest of the public. So, we want to fly you to England first, you are an Ambassador for Freemasonary, visiting various lodges wherever you go, we want you to promote Freemasonary and set up an exchange system for Freemasons to visit Australia and we Freemasons can travel the world in peace and harmony. Yes Tiny, we will not let Freemasonary be used politically, but you are a Sergeant in the Police Force, so you are working for the Police Force, not a political party. We need this man back in Australia.'

Peter Smith then spoke 'A few months ago 15 military rifles disappeared out of a factory warehouse, that is not unusual, but it is the weapon that concern us, it has many characteristics, but we won't go into that, if this weapon is dismantled into two pieces we cannot see it at border security in airports. it doesn't show up on any radar screen, what it is made of, is the worry, its parts may be the handle on a suitcase, or a wheel on the suitcase, cigarette case, glasses case, so we need to get one in order to sort out the problem. So, we need you to purchase five or more of these military rifles through Mr Dude.'

The man from ASIO said, 'He is too slick for us to actually pin anything on him; he keeps his hands clean, so Tiny, he is a slippery customer.'

He handed me a large envelope, this is everything we know about this weapon and the photos. You are not an acting placement in Europe, but MI5 is working with you.' He handed me another large envelope. 'These are all your documents, and your credit card. Your ticket has been booked on the plane for this afternoon. Anything we've forgotten will be in the envelopes.'

I looked at the Grand Secretary. 'You told me I was in trouble, but not how deep, and you have locked me into this. How do I explain this to others?'

'You are on long service leave, Tiny, and enjoying your craft. Now in this little, beautifully made briefcase, you have all the papers you will need for your credibility. Oh, I nearly forgot, Joyce will take care of your dog, Jack.'

At the airport, I checked my bags in, put his passport and papers in front of the man at the desk, the man smiled. 'G'day Tiny, and where are you off to?'

I looked up to see an old companion. 'I thought you were still in the police force?'

'No, Tiny, I left a couple of months ago, got a job here, too much paperwork and politics in the Police Force. I enjoyed being a police officer, but not all the paperwork.' He looked at my papers, whoever booked you in wasn't very intelligent, how are you going to sit in a seat in cattle class with your legs, just a moment.' He picked up the phone and spoke to somebody. 'Yes, he is 6' 5" tall, with long legs. He is also a police sergeant; his ticket has been booked by the department. Thank you for that,' and hung up the receiver.

'Tiny you are now in Business Class, your seat is by the emergency door, and you will have plenty of leg room, you have also been booked in as premium, You're a valued customer, go to gate 8 and have a good flight, Tiny.'

I winked at him and nodded, I went through customs, took off my watch, belt and necklace, put them in a tray with my man bag, I went through the machine, walked through the arch of love, nothing happened, I picked up all my things off of the tray, put my belt back on, and my necklace, a man with a people transport vehicle asked me if I would like to hop on. 'Sir, we will take you down to the lounge.'

I didn't argue; I got on. I was ushered down some steps into a lounge. A hostess said to me. 'Mr Harrison, we will call you when your flight is ready. There are complimentary wines and spirits if you wish. Also, there is beer in the fridge, and if you would like to take a plate to the buffet and help yourself.'

'Thank you very much.' I thought I must do this more often. I sat down in an armchair and sipped my wine, ate my fresh ham and cheese bread roll, and tried to relax. All I could think about was Jack. Yes, Joyce will look after Jack; I will miss him.

The hostess startled me. 'Your flight is ready, sir, if you would follow me.'

I walked down a corridor onto the plane and was shown my seat by a flight attendant. 'Sir, this is the emergency door. Are you able to get up and open it?'

'Yes, I am.'

In an emergency, push this up, turn the handle, let the handle go, and the door will open, and if it is needed, an emergency chute will automatically come out. Thank you, sir.'

I sat down in the comfortable armchair. Hey Jack, this is more comfortable than your $600 chair. I was handed a complimentary glass of wine. A man sat down next to me, the seat belt went on, and before I knew it, we were in the air. What am I doing here? What is in store for me? Mine is not to wonder why, just do it, but what?

CHAPTER 5

I STRETCHED MY legs out and sipped my wine; it was good quality. Joyce would love this. The man in the seat next to me put out his hand and said, 'My name is Trevor.'

I put out my hand and said, 'They call me Tiny.'

'Where's your destination, Tiny?'

'England.'

'Then we'll both be going to the same place. All my relatives live in England. I miss them. My parents were £10 Poms.'

I grinned. 'I'm true blue, bred in Australia, I'm taking part of my long service leave.'

We chatted for a while, then our food arrived. Not much, but it was good; I enjoyed it. After that, I fell off to sleep, a deep sleep.

We eventually landed in Singapore. I looked out of the window and was fascinated by the number of ships at anchor in the bay.

Trevor told me they're all waiting for a cargo to go somewhere in the world. They pay off the captain and crew, and a Singaporean stays on as her caretaker. I was also astounded by the number of aircraft at Changi International Airport. We disembarked and stretched our legs. As I stood up, Trevor said, 'Now I know why they call you Tiny!' He winked.

I walked down to the foyer with Trevor. We found the big ponds; they had enormous koi fish swimming in them. We both went and had a coffee until it was time to re-board our plane, and we were on our way to England.

I browsed through the paperwork I had been given, then looked at the statistics of the firearms. What they were capable of was very disturbing. One bullet fired, no sound, just a click, click. Different bullets, different capabilities: laser beams, telescopic sights, heat detectors. Being able to see a target through a wall. And this weapon could not be seen on radar, incredible. It could be stripped down into many parts so that customs could not detect it. On its stock and barrel there is a stabbing blade, neatly hidden. It could be equipped with a grenade launcher. Nasty bit of work in the wrong hands. There was a lot more information, but it was beyond me to really understand. I put the paperwork back into its envelope. Then I started to go through the file on Mr Dude. To anyone looking for him, he was a ghost, moving quickly from one place to another. From one country to another. Using others to hide, he never actually did any of the dirty work; he used a go-between. From the seller to the buyer of weapons, drugs, ivory, and any other commodity that would make money. It is said that he does not get involved in human trafficking. Cross him, and you are dead, never to be seen again. His personality is made of ice!

Trevor's voice startled me. 'Are you alright, Tiny? You look like you've seen the Devil himself!'

I looked at Trevor for a moment, not saying anything, trying to get it all together in my mind. 'Yes, Trevor, you could say that. I'm going to order a drink.'

I put my hand up, and the flight attendant said, 'Can I help you, sir?'

'Yes, could I please have a double scotch?'

'Certainly, sir.'

My right hand wasn't shaking, but I held in just in case. Just what had they got me involved in? The flight attendant turned up with my drink; I took it and said, 'Thank you.' She turned to walk away; I swallowed the drink straight down.

Trevor said, 'Is there anything I can do to help you, Tiny?'

'Thank you all the same, Trevor, but I've gotta to sort this out for myself.'

He looked at me with a puzzled expression on his face. Then he said, 'Tiny, we're not going anywhere. How about another double scotch?'

I smiled at him. 'Yes, I think that might help.' Trevor ordered two double scotches. He talked about England, and what he missed most, and the weather. It was something like small talk; it was just what I needed to put my mind back into perspective.

Once again food turned up, and I enjoyed it. The fruit with ice cream seemed to settle me down. I wanted to read through my Masonic papers, but they were in my suitcase.

I leaned back in my comfortable chair and closed my eyes. My grandchildren appeared in my mind, each one with their different personalities, laughing and giggling, and Jack, my dog, playing with them. He knew how to play with each one, be it rough or gentle, or just totally submitting with them. I thought of Joyce, my dear friend, just sitting there next to me, letting me know what I had to do, just reminding me. I had fallen back into a deep sleep; I awoke to the sound of the flight attendant's voice. 'Your breakfast, sir.' I blinked my eyes and slightly shook my head, trying to get my mind together again.

'Thank you.' I took the tray. Bacon and scrambled eggs, a bowl of fruit, and coffee. I grinned at Trevor. 'Hope I didn't keep you awake with my snoring.'

'No, Tiny, I was too busy listening to my own snoring.'

The seat belt light went on; I put it on and looked out of the window. We seemed to be following the Thames River towards London. Then a voice came through on the intercom.

'This is the captain speaking. We're going to go into a holding platform until we obtain permission to land, so we will be flying in a circle waiting for the permission. Sit back and enjoy the view.'

We were flying down alongside London, we could see the Thames River, the Tower of London, the bridges across the Thames, The London Eye, Buckingham Palace, Battersea Power Station, then we were turning over to the countryside, beautiful green fields like a quilt, then houses neatly in rows.

The captain's voice came back on the intercom. 'Ladies and gentlemen, we now have permission to land. I sincerely hope you have enjoyed your flight. On behalf of myself and my crew, we thank you for flying with us.'

We were flying low over some houses, then over factories, and now we were down on the runway. Before I could get my mind together, we were disembarking and picking up our suitcases.

CHAPTER 6

THE CUSTOMS OFFICER looked at my passport. 'You are on long service leave?'

'Yes, I am.'

'Go through Mr Harrison, enjoy your holiday.'

I pushed my trolley out into the arrivals hall. Where now? Three men walked up to me. The first man put his hand out, and as he shook my hand, he said, 'Welcome to England, Mr Harrison.' He gave me the Masonic handshake. 'I am Terry, Master of the London Lodge. This gentleman is Michael; he is the Treasurer of the Lodge.'

We shook hands. 'A pleasure to meet you, Mr Harrison.'

'And this gentleman is Pedro; he is our Almoner.'

We shook hands; he put his other hand on top of mine. 'It is a pleasure, Mr Harrison, to have a distinguished Australian Freemason visiting our Lodges.'

I replied. 'It is a great honour to be here visiting you in England, and please call me Tiny; everybody else does.'

They all looked at me and smiled. Pedro said, 'We have arranged accommodation for you and will pick you up tomorrow.'

The Lodge meeting is our largest, and you will be our distinguished guest.

I was taken to a guesthouse in London. It was a bit fancier than I was used to, but this is England, and it was very English. A young man took my bags up to my room, and I followed him. He opened the door and gave me the key, then he put my suitcases in the room. I glanced around the room, very, very nice. A very nice British sitting room. What I could see of the bed, it looked very comfortable. There was a bathroom on one side. The young man asked me, 'If there's anything you require, sir, please call me.'

'Could we get an understanding, please call me Tiny, not sir, because in Australia we are all equal.' He frowned at me. 'No, you wouldn't understand; you would have to come to Australia. Visit us to find out.'

He raised his eyebrows. 'Well, Tiny, there are two gentlemen in the lounge waiting to talk to you. I do not know who they are, and my name is Jarrett.'

'Okay, Jarrett, could you please get me a mug of coffee? In Australia, we call it a flat white, with two sugars and just a little bit of milk, and I would like it in the lounge, please.'

I walked into the lounge, saw the two gentlemen, and went up to introduce myself.

'Good morning gentlemen, I am Tiny Harrison.'

They both stood up. The first man shook my hand. He had an angry grip. 'Sir John Moore Tiny, and this is my colleague Andrew Fraser from MI5.'

We shook hands again, the same angry hand grip; we all sat down, and coffee was brought to us in mugs.

Sir John said, 'Ah, coffee Australian style, good man. Tiny, you know why you have been brought to England?'

'Yes, I do Sir John.'

'Well, we are here to back you up whenever we can. We have a list of places for you to go to enquire about the Dude. First, you will go to Freddy's Nightclub in Soho.

He doesn't sell drugs, and he doesn't sell contraband; he gives information.'

'Tell me, Sir John, why me? Why not one of your own people?'

'We tried one of our own, but we shot ourselves in the foot. We sent what we call an aristocrat, we didn't have a choice. Like you, we are just pawns in the game.'

'Well, Sir John, where is that man now?'

'Because he comes from the upper class, he was sent back to us, a little bruised and with one fingernail missing. You Tiny are a totally different type of man; you will not try to play games with them, you're playing it straight.'

The man from MI5 said, 'That is your personality Tiny, you couldn't do it any different. In this envelope, there are the addresses where you are to go and get the information on each one.' He picked up another envelope. 'If you are sent to Paris, there is another list.' He handed me the second list.

He picked up another envelope. 'And here is a little bit of sugar to sweeten up people with information; some is in English, others in French. If you need more, we will provide it.'

Sir John said, 'Give me your watch and take this one; they looked identical. If you need us, just pull the winder out three times and we will know exactly where you are. Talk to the phone; it will not answer, but we will hear you.'

I took the other watch, picked up my coffee and sipped it, trying to think of something to say, going over what they had said, 'I don't think I have any questions at the moment gentlemen, but I don't like the games we're playing. I would prefer to be sitting on the fence with you two gentlemen. Now if you would excuse me, I have jet lag, and I need to shut my eyes.'

Sir John said, 'We perfectly understand Tiny. Do not phone Australia, your safety is important to us, and the less they know the better.'

CHAPTER 7

THE NEXT THING I knew, my bedside phone was ringing. I picked it up. 'Good evening, Mr Harrison, it is reception here. Will you be coming down for tea or having tea in your room?'

'I will come down, thank you.'

After I had my tea, I returned to my room and went back to bed.

I awoke at 6 am, had a quick shower, and went for a walk in the nearby park. I missed my dog, Jack. On my return, I had a really good full English breakfast: bacon, eggs, sausages, tomatoes, and toast with chunky marmalade.

Jarrett, the receptionist said, 'Good morning, Tiny, did you enjoy your breakfast?'

'Yes. Jarrett, I did.'

'A message has come for you, Tiny. A car will pick you up at 11 am, dinner suit and full regalia.

'Thanks Jarrett.'

I walked into the foyer at 10.55 am, and there was Terry waiting.

'Good morning, Tiny. We're off to the circus.'

I followed him out to the car. The other two gentlemen were sitting in the back seat. Terry said, 'Don't worry about those vagabonds in the back seat; any trouble and I will put them in the boot.'

I said G'day to both of them and settled into the front seat.

Michael, the Treasurer, said, 'It is a nice guesthouse, one of the best.'

'Yes, I thoroughly agree.'

Terry spoke. 'Will you be doing a talk in the South?'

'Yes, Terry, if I could.'

The large temple was very impressive. We walked up the steps, passing the two columns and entering the big doors, through to the foyer. I was surprised to see a bar serving drinks. 'What would you like to drink, Tiny?'

'Just a glass of white wine, please.'

After I drank my wine and the others finished their drinks, we went into the Lodge. A few others waited outside the door. I was very impressed with all the aprons hanging on either side of the walls; they were from all over the world. I looked at all the names on a big board of Masters. One said Christopher O'Hara, I grinned to myself. Chris was my 2IC in Australia. I checked out the date alongside the name, 1831, that would be about right! I've never asked him his age, now I know! I heard the knock on the door.

'Open,' and a voice said, 'whom have you there?'

Another voice said, 'A number of Past Masters.'

'Halt, while I report to the Worshipful Master.'

Then the door opened, and we were let in; the door closed behind us. To my surprise, they were halfway through the ceremony. The Lodge was closed; some men went to the toilet, others had a quick drink at the bar. Then the Lodge was reopened, and we ceased pleasure and went back to work; the ceremony continued.

Later in the South, we had an excellent meal. I gave my talk on the Fellowship of Freemasonary. The South closed in Love and Harmony, then everybody started to leave. The caterers were cleaning up, ready for the next Lodge at 7 pm.

I asked Terry how many Lodges meet here a day; he replied two or three a day.

On our way home in the car, we dropped off the other two gentlemen at their homes.

I asked Terry, "Do you know where Freddy's Nightclub is in Soho?'

He gave me a funny look. 'Why would you want to go to Freddy's? I wouldn't have thought it was your type of entertainment.'

'No, it's not normally, but I have to talk to Freddy, and I can only see him at 6 pm when the club opens.'

Terry gave me a cheeky grin. 'On our way, Tiny, hold on tight.'

There was good parking, and we were the early birds; we both walked up to the bar. The man behind the bar looked at us with a puzzled expression. Two customers wearing dinner suits and Masonic badges on their lapels. He said to us, 'Gentlemen, I would suggest you take off your bow ties and your Masonic badges, I wouldn't wear mine because I was taught to be cautious. Now, what can I do for your gentlemen?'

I said, 'My friend Terry here would like a drink, and I put a £50 note on the bar, and I believe you would have one also.'

Terry didn't hesitate. 'Double scotch, neat.'

'Is Freddy available?'

The barman said, 'I was a copper once, and I believe you are a copper as well.'

I grinned. 'You must have been good; I'm a Sergeant in the Australian Police Force. Let's just say I'm on long service leave.'

He winked at me, picked up his mobile phone. 'Freddy, this will make your day, there are two Freemasons here, one is a Sergeant in the Australian Police Force.' We heard the voice on the other end of the phone.

'You're an idiot; pull the other leg.'

'You see that office over there, with the glass around it? He's in there. Tell him you have come to pull the other leg.'

We had by now removed our Masonic badges and bow ties. I put my hand on Terry's shoulder. 'This meeting could be a little bit delicate. Enjoy your drink, and if you want another one, I don't know.'

I thanked the barman and walked over to the office, knocked on the door. A very broad Cockney voice said, 'If you don't want to waste my time, go away.'

The door opened; a big man stood in the doorway. His eyes seemed to be scanning me in a way I didn't like. His fists were clenched tight. You don't tangle with this type of man on your own. He bent his head down to look at me and said, 'I don't like bloody coppers.'

A voice behind him said, 'Let him in, Bruiser.'

The man didn't hesitate, but stepped aside. As I walked in, I looked him straight in the eyes and, with my most serious face, said, 'Good evening, Bruiser,' and walked up to the desk. 'Good evening, Freddy. My name is Tiny Harrison, and yes, I'm a police officer in the Australian Police Force.'

Freddy gestured to the other chair, extending his hand out flat. 'Excuse my man, he lets people know where he stands with me.' He paused for a moment. 'Treat him with respect. Now, what do you want?'

I thought for a moment, talk to him straight. 'I'm looking for a man they call The Dude.'

He didn't say anything for a few moments; he just stared at me. Then said, 'I don't mix in those circles, I don't deal drugs, or any other contraband, but because you are an Australian and I've learned to respect Australians, I will warn you, don't get involved with him, he's bad stuff, and he plays rough.'

'Freddy, I'm working for the Australian Government, and I need your help.'

'Tiny, you are the typical Australian, no messing about, straight to the point.' He picked up his mobile phone and rang a number. 'Freddy here, put me through to Alan. Oh, so he's in a meeting. Would you want me to send the Bruiser around and have a little talk with you? Now, put Alan on the phone and stop the bullshit.'

Alan answered the phone. 'Alan, I have an Australian here; he's in the Australian Police Force, working for the Australian Government. I do not know what he wants, but he wants to talk to the Dude.'

There was silence on the phone, then Alan said, 'It's gonna cost him. What's his name?'

'He is known by the name of Tiny Harrison.'

'Why do they all come up with these stupid names for cover!'

He put out his hand. 'Your passport and warrant card, please.'

I gave them to him; he spoke on the phone again. 'On his warrant card it says Ronald Harrison Sergeant, on his passport it says Ronald Harrison, he's tall, about 6 feet 5 inches tall, that's why they call him Tiny Harrison. Yes, yes, got all that. I wouldn't have rung you, but he's Australian, don't have any choice, do I?' he closed his mobile phone.

'Tiny, you, I and Bruiser are going out to lunch at the Twin Anchors Pub. The owner, who we call Fancy Pants, calls it a restaurant. You are buying us lunch.'

I replied, 'That will be my pleasure Freddy, thank you for your help.' I winked at him. 'Now, I'll get out of your hair.'

'Tiny, be here at 10.30 am tomorrow. Now go and have a drink at the bar.'

I shook his hand, turned to walk towards the door, then it hit me! The Bruiser. I put my finger up to the Bruiser, slightly moved it. 'You were a boxer.' His face lit up like a beacon.

'Yes, I was, and I was the best.'

I put my hand out and shook his hand; I put my other hand on his shoulder. 'Yes, you were the best. Can I buy you a drink?'

'Thanks, but no, I'm on these tablets.'

I smiled at him and went back to the bar. 'A double scotch, one piece of ice, please. How's your drink, Terry?' He put his empty glass forward, and they were filled again.

'Terry, would you like to stay awhile?'

Terry had a silly grin all over his face. 'Tiny, I thought you'd never ask.'

CHAPTER 8

THE NEXT MORNING I arrived at Freddy's Nightclub at 10.30 am. My eyes were a little heavy, my forehead a little tight; I gritted my teeth. But I'm glad Terry enjoyed himself, and I hope he feels the same way as I do.

Freddy and I climbed into the back of his Mercedes; the Bruiser drove. Freddy said, 'Don't normally come to this toffee-nosed area, they are all would Be's. Could Be's, with fingers up their @#$ and turn up at my club.'

We pulled up in front of the Twin Anchors Restaurant; it had certainly been jazzed up with fancy awnings and flower pots. The facade was painted red and blue. We got out of the car, and another man drove it away and parked it. A gentleman walked out of the door, extremely well-dressed. Freddy said to him. 'You don't look very well, Alan.'

'You being here, Freddy, doesn't make me feel comfortable.'

His eyes were working me over, trying to sort me out for himself. Then he looked at Bruiser. 'Behave yourself Bruiser, this is my place, not Freddy's.'

Bruiser replied, 'Nice to meet you too, Alan. I should have looked after you better at school.'

I thought, I wonder if Alan treated all his customers the same?

We followed him through the door. Customers sitting at their tables glanced at Freddy, but quickly put their eyes back down to the table, not wanting their guests to know that they know Freddy. Freddy was enjoying himself; he would stop briefly at a table. 'Hello Timothy, how's the clothing business going? See you on Saturday, will we?'

We walked past another table; the same thing happened. 'Hello Mary, your mum and dad doing well, are they? Catch up with you later.'

He walked to another table, six people were sitting around it. He put his hands on one of the men's shoulders. You could see the man stiffen up, see how nervous he was. All his guests were looking at him. Freddy said to me, 'This man is the best; I hope he climbs the political ladder to the top.'

Then Alan said, 'Your table is ready, Freddy; come and join us.'

We all sat down. The table had a beautiful green tablecloth and a small vase of flowers in the centre. The chairs were quite impressive and comfortable, with arms.

Alan said, 'I don't want you to get the wrong impression between Freddy and me. He picked me up off the streets as a kid, and he and his wife brought me up. I found this pub and wanted to buy it. It was very run-down and didn't suit this area. Freddy gave me the finances, and I had to pay him back, no interest. Payment started when I opened this restaurant. We play our own particular game to keep our business separate, and the customers do sometimes get a little confused.'

A lady walked out of the kitchen and mingled around the tables, talking to the guests. Then she walked up behind Bruiser and threw her arms around his neck and kissed him on the cheek. I'll never forget the smile on his face.

'Tiny, this is my wife, Nancy; she is the chef. Bruiser takes her shopping every Tuesday in the Mercedes. Now, Tiny, to business. The gentleman you are looking for lives on different levels to us. We're down here,' he put his hand on the table, 'we are just the @#$% pawns in their game. They are up there.' He put his hand up in the air. 'They can snuff you out in the blink of an eye. When they have finished with you, walk away. Don't interfere or get involved in any way.' He slid a piece of paper over to me and pointed to the writing. 'You are booked into this hotel in Paris, France. You have been booked on the

Eurostar train first thing tomorrow morning. Please do not get me involved anymore. I've only done this for Freddy.'

Nancy, his wife, said, 'Freddy, if this backfires on us, you will be in my frying pan.' Bruiser raised his eyebrows and said, 'Who who.'

CHAPTER 9

THE NEXT MORNING, I was walking to the foyer carrying my suitcase. As I got to reception, Jarrett turned his back to me and said, 'What you don't see, you don't know.'

I placed the keys to my room on his desk and took the hint.

I boarded the Eurostar train and sat down in my allocated seat, it was extremely comfortable. The train left the platform so smoothly, if you weren't looking out of the window, you wouldn't have known you were moving. It picked up speed so smoothly, a waiter offered me a glass of wine, which I didn't decline, even though it was very early in the morning, I sat there sipping the wine, I was fascinated by the speed with which we were travelling. It seemed very strange trying to watch the scenery, we were moving too fast to see the scenery close up; you had to look at the distance. Then we were going through the channel under the sea, next thing I knew we had popped back out into the sunlight and were in France. We soon pulled into Paris. I stood behind another man waiting to go through customs; he started to argue with the customs officer. 'I don't have to put up with all this @#$%.'

The customs officer put up his finger, and before you could blink, he was being marched away by two police officers, heavily armed...I thought, behave yourself Tiny, I put my passport down in front of the officer. 'What is your business in France Mr Harrison?'

'I'm on long service leave; I will be sightseeing.'

He looked down at my suitcase, my Masonic case, and my man bag. He very briefly gave the Masonic sign of Fidelity; I did the same. He smiled. 'Enjoy yourself, Mr Harrison.'

I got into a taxi and went straight to my hotel. My room was quite large, a beautifully furnished lounge with a big dining table, there were big bay windows letting in plenty of light. This will be very comfortable. I put my bags in the bedroom, got out my Masonic papers, found the Lodge I wanted and the Secretary's number, I rang the number and a voice said, 'Bonjour.'

I told the voice that I was sorry, but I didn't speak French, I'm from Australia and my name is Tiny Harrison and I was looking for the secretary of the Lodge.

'I am he.'

'Is it possible to visit your lodge? I am a Freemason.'

'Yes, yes Mr Harrison, we have a Lodge meeting this evening, if you could give me your address, I will have you picked up at 4.30 pm.'

I gave him the address of my hotel.

'We will be very pleased to receive you in our Lodge, we are doing a second degree.'

'Thank you, I will look forward to it.'

He chuckled. 'It will be in French, but I think you will understand. Au revoir.' We hung up.

Later that afternoon I once again stood at the entrance of a Lodge, with others waiting their turn to enter, the Tyler let us through the door, and I was presented to the Worshipful Master, as a visitor from Australia.

The meal in the South was excellent, a little bit different, but as we would say, damn good tucker.

I was returned to my hotel about 10.30 pm. I opened the door to my room and put my bag and case down, to my surprise and annoyance there were two men standing there.

'In a loud, sharp voice I yelled. 'Get out of my room,'

One man stepped forward, he raised his right hand and was about to slap me in the face. I lifted my left arm up to block his right arm, thrusting my right arm forward and with an open hand hit him hard on the side of his nose. He staggered backwards, holding his nose, I could see the blood through his fingers.

A very Husky, gravelly voice said, 'Stop now!'

The other man stood aside, and I was looking at a man sitting on one of the dining room chairs, he gestured to the chair in front of him. I didn't argue, I just sat down on it. We sat for a minute, not saying anything. He was sorting me up, and thinking deeply. I also studied him, pin striped suit, well cut, and what I would have thought was a silk shirt, grey shoes. I looked at his shoelaces carefully. You could tell if a person was right or left-handed by the way the shoelaces were tied.

He was wearing a Krueger hat, looking at it closely it appeared to have been made specifically for him, it was silk with a silk grey band. He was wearing the hat slightly forward over his forehead, which hid some of his features. He kept his knees together and held a cane, which he held upright. He had his two hands on top of it, the left hand on top. His left-hand thumb was gently rubbing the index finger. Was this nerves, or a way of thinking? Ears were level. His face, a normal face, neither fat nor thin.

'Mr Harrison, you have summed me up as a policeman would, and you have made a statement, do you see the red dot on your left breast?'

I looked down at my breast; there was a red dot. I froze for a moment, a sense of fear went through me. I slowly turned my head and looked out of the window, I could see the sniper in the opposite building. I looked back at him, I assumed this was the infamous Dude, I gave him the coldest look I could, not letting him see my fear.

'Now Mr Harrison, down to business.'

'As you know I am a Police Sergeant, not a Politician, or a spy. The Commissioner of Police in Victoria gave me this task to do, which I don't like. If you could pass me my bag, there are documents in it.' The big man picked up my bag and my Masonic briefcase. First of all he put my Masonic briefcase down in front of him, turning it around so that the handle was facing away from him, he opened it. Quickly browsed through it, then he closed it. He undid the zip on my man bag taking out the envelopes and a few of my personal items, but he didn't find what he was really looking for, a weapon. He looked through the first envelope, which were my Masonic addresses, then he opened the larger envelope and took out the papers, he looked at them briefly, then handed them to the Dude. 'My superior's have been informed that fifteen of these weapons were mislaid in a factory warehouse, where? That is unknown to them. They want to purchase five of these weapons.'

The Dude slowly read through the documents, studying them very carefully. He scrolled through them again, he was looking for something. He turned over to the last page, then turned it over again, looking at the blank sheet on the back, he took off the clip and handed it to the big fella who walked over to the table lamp, he took the shade off of the lamp, then held the piece of paper over the light bulb, with the writing facing down, so he was looking at light reflecting through it. He nodded to the Dude, and gave him back the piece of paper.

The Dude stared at it for a minute or two, thinking. 'Yes, Mr Harrison, we have the rest of the information we require, in four days I will be at the entrance to the Vatican, do not leave, wait, that will be Friday, I will keep the documents. The meeting is over.'

I felt the coldness in this man. He stood up very easily, then walked to the bathroom.

I said to myself for my own amusement. At least that part of him is normal.

'Mr Harrison stay in that chair for the next ten minutes.' I looked down at the red dot, and didn't say anything. They left, or should I say, they just seemed to disappear.

CHAPTER 10

I LOOKED AT my watch, it was just past midnight, I was tired and worried. Put it all to bed Tiny, and sort it out in the morning. I went to bed and awoke with a start, I sat straight up. Was yesterday just a dream? I got up and had a shower, got dressed and walked into the lounge, my Masonic briefcase was closed, but not locked, my other papers were still on the table. I put them back into my bag. I felt that the room was crowding in on me, I had to get out, I walked down to a park and sat down on a park bench, I looked at the green grass, the trees gently swaying in the breeze, ducks and other birds were feeding on the grass. The pond was very beautiful and majestic. I felt alone, why am I here, what have they done to me, just then I saw a man walking his dog, the dog looked similar to my dog, I wanted to pet him, to stroke him, and yes, to give him a cuddle. Tears formed in my eyes. Where are you Joyce, I need you to be here, to be with me and advise me where to go next. I got my handkerchief out and whipped my eyes. You're a fool Harrison, you're not alone. You will be with 80 Freemasons. Brothers, any one of them would be with you now if you called him.

I put my handkerchief back in my pocket, stood up and went back to the restaurant in the hotel. A waiter came up to my table, and I ordered bacon, eggs, sausage and onions. 'One coffee, in a mug, in Australia we call it a flat white, two sugars please.'

The waiter said, 'we make sure.'

I sat listening to the chatter in the restaurant, noisy lot, the French, they sounded like my galahs at home when I haven't fed them, and they're waiting for their breakfast.

A man walked up to my table. 'Excuse me Sir, I'm the Manager, are you free today?'

I replied. 'Yes Sir, I am.'

'We have a coach trip going to the Dom Perignon winery today, would you like to go?'

'Yes, I would.'

'We would have to put it on your account, if you would like to get your belongings and wait here in the restaurant, we will fetch you.'

'Thank you, I'll enjoy that.'

The coach driver looked at me and winked, if you'd like to sit here in the front seat, there will be more leg room, more than there was in the South!'

I smiled. 'I didn't notice the food was so damn good.'

He smiled again, and went to the next passenger. We were ready to leave and he picked up his microphone. 'Bonjour, good morning, I know we've got one Dinky Dye Australian on board, a couple of Yanks, and just to make it more interesting, I'd say one or two English people. Our interpreter here, and he gestured to a lady, now the biggest problem is, she only speaks Japanese, but I'm quite sure she'll sort it out, please sit back and enjoy yourselves.

Our tour guide introduced herself. 'My name is Maria. And our driver, he's a wonderful man, we have worked together for quite some number of years, and we get on so well, we never argue, I think so much of him that I let down all the tyres on his car. Now, I may repeat myself twice, so that you understand what I'm trying to say, for the sake of the Australian sitting at the front here.' she pointed her finger down to my head, and then gently patted it.

The driver said, 'That's funny, I don't own a car, I only have a motorbike.'

A voice at the back of the bus yelled out. 'Aussie, Aussie, Aussie.' I put my thumb up in the air. Somebody else shouted out. 'How did two of them get through the net?'

The journey started off with laughter. But I realised Maria had an Australian accent.

We drove past many special landmarks and scenery, but eventually we arrived at the city of Reims, sacred place of

Joan of Arc. You can see her statue, they call it Joanie on her pony. As a young child she could talk to heaven, in her teens she spoke to the Pope, she said she could save France from its enemies. The Pope playing politics gave her an army, she won many battles. The British did not like it, how does a girl teenager win so many battles? Also the Pope didn't like the popularity she had with the people. Joan was tried in a court of law. The Pope and the English twisted it to suit themselves, The British took over and she was burnt at the stake, she wasn't given a cross or blessing from clergymen, and her ashes were thrown into the river, so that there wasn't anything for her followers to come and visit and worship.

The coach pulled up alongside the statue of Joannie on her pony. Maria said, 'The toilets are to your left, there's a lady inside who looks after the toilets, they call her the dragon lady, she has been there a long time and is paid by the fee she charges.'

The women lined up for the toilets, the men went straight in, when the men were nearly finished, the dragon lady asked the women to enter the mens toilets with a scowl on her face that you didn't argue with.

After our break we all went into the Cathedral, then returned to the coach. We headed for the winery looking at many things on the way. Maria pointed out a small castle on a hill, she said, 'The castle was built by the Knights Templar to protect the pilgrims when they were visiting Jerusalem.

I thought the Yarra Valley and Adelaide had plenty of vineyards, not as many as I was seeing here, they were everywhere, we eventually turned up at the famous Dom Perignon Vineyard, and were ushered into a very large room, it was very old, the monks offered us glasses of wine. I thought of Joyce, she would so much have enjoyed this, it was her world. A lady stepped forward. 'I am Jornette, I will be your tour guide for today, we are now going to take you down into the cellars of the winery, and show you how it's made, where it's stored, there are so many tunnels, that we don't know exactly how many, because so many have been sealed up to protect them from looters, during the last two wars Hitler would have sold Napoleon Brandies for credit or exchange it for oil.

We walked through tunnels looking at the pictures on the walls of wines, but all the walls to the side of the main one looked exactly the same, they were well hidden.

We watched people turning the bottles, some ¼ of the way and others half way, we watched others holding the bottle to the light to examine it for its quality, watched the grapes being crushed and stored. We were ushered into another large room for a tasting of champagnes and other wines. I didn't really like champagne, but I could learn to. I could have drunk this all night with Joyce and a few friends.

Eventually we returned to the coach, but when I walked out into the light I did have to put my hand on the wall to steady myself, but it did feel good.

I don't remember much of the journey back to the hotel!

CHAPTER 11

THE NEXT DAY I boarded the train for Rome, I was very impressed with the train, I couldn't get enough of the scenery and the history of everything, all the Tuscany villages on top of the hillsides. I kept asking myself how old are they, what is there history. If I had my campervan Jack and Joyce and I could be content just to travel through Italy, Spain and Greece. Eventually we arrived in Rome, and I took a taxi to my hotel.

I woke up the next morning at 7 am, and got myself ready for another day, there is nothing like a good breakfast to prepare you for the unexpected.

I have this day to myself, I've always wanted to see the Colosseum, and walk around it. I was totally fascinated by the size and the age of it, the engineering was incredible, and the stone masonry. But what I couldn't make out were the holes in the stonework, it looked like somebody had been firing at it with a Canon. There was a sign that said information, with a young lady wearing a uniform standing next to it. I asked her what caused the holes in the stonework. She said that when they built the Colosseum they put lead bars between the stones anchoring them together, so when there was an earthquake the lead bars held everything together, in the early days lead was very valuable, and it was looted. That is why part of the Colosseum wall had collapsed.

I must have spent four hours wandering around, it was fascinating history, which you could not deny. I was getting weary so found a coffee shop what sold food as well, I sat down at a small table and ordered coffee and some food. I was enjoying watching people sightseeing. A young lady, maybe about 19, very hard to tell these days, she held out a plastic cup to me, and looked at me with pleading eyes, obviously she wanted money. I had been warned about the gypsies, and told not to give them money. I asked her. 'Do you understand English?' she nodded. 'I have to work to get money, I buy things with that money.' I pointed to a small stone on the ground. 'Pick up the stone and give it to me.' She looked at me puzzled. But she picked up the stone and gave it to me. 'Now, I can take this stone home and remember Rome.' I put three coins in her plastic cup, she stood staring at me and started to walk away, then stopped, turned around and looked at me again, giving me a puzzled look, then she walked away.

A man sitting at the next table gave a small chuckle. 'Well, I've never seen that before, but I believe she understood the point you made. The older ones before her, used to make up small trinkets, the younger ones beg for money and give nothing back for it, they are non statistics in Rome, but the government tolerate them, and so does the general society. Tourists keep them alive through their begging. But this is Rome, and every city has its problems.' He got up from his table and walked away. I noticed there wasn't a coffee cup on the table or anything else.

I felt a little bit tired and weary so went back to the hotel. I laid on the bed, put my head on the pillow and was asleep.

I woke just on daylight, got out of bed and walked over to the window and watched the sun rising over Rome. Another memory I will never forget.

I made two cups of coffee, one after the other, or, one before the other. I didn't feel like breakfast, it definitely wasn't nerves, I said to myself, idiot.

I picked up my man bag, and my map of Rome. The Trevi fountain is about a five minute walk, it will be something to take my mind off the rest of the day. Because I got up early, there was hardly anybody there, I took a coin out of my pocket, turned around, and threw if into the fountain, being here was far better than any photo, the beauty of it took your breath away. We don't have anything like this in Australia, we may have Uluru, but that is nature, this is one mans creation so long ago, his interpretation of heaven and water.

It was quite easy getting a cab at this time of the morning, I got into the back of a cab and opened up the map of Rome, the driver looked in his rear view mirror, so I could see his eyes. 'The Vatican please.'

He asked me. 'Have you been to Rome before?'

'No, but I've got the map.' looking at his eyes, that wasn't the answer he wanted. We arrived at the Vatican, I handed the driver a note, he looked at it, and grinned.

'Yes, buddy, everybody has to make a quid to survive.'

I got out of the cab, and put the strap over my head, with the bag in front of me, with my arm over it, that's nice and comfy, I patted my bag, you will be safe there. I stood looking at the courtyard and the ring of columns surrounding it. My mind went quiet, why? I'm trying to take it all in. do I walk straight across the courtyard to the front entrance of the Vatican? No, I think that would make me feel arrogant. I will walk around it through the columns. My mind was still in a state of limbo looking at all the columns, all tall and majestic, each one make its own statement. I got to the big doors at the entrance to the Vatican, looked at my watch, I have time, I walked in, I could not go right in, for there was security. Looking at the Vatican I asked myself, have they built this to God, or were they making a statement, we are the closest to God, who knows? To me a newborn child is the closest to God, it doesn't know hate, or animosity, only love. I stood by the entrance waiting, a security officer tactfully asked me a question, in Italian. I said, 'English please.'

He replied. 'Can I help you Sir?'

'No thank you, I'm waiting for a friend.'

He kept on walking, I waited but could hear music and singing from inside the Vatican, it was very relaxing. I was a little startled when a boy about 15 years of age, said to me 'You are Tiny Harrison?'

'Yes, I am.'

'You come with me.'

We went back through the columns, eventually walking down the main road, then left, another road, I couldn't pronounce the name, we turned right into a smaller road, these were very old buildings, definitely from the early Roman era. The young boy pointed to a narrow lane, I could only just put my elbows up on either side. He said to me 'You walk up there.'

I didn't argue with him, but turned and started walking, it was a steep climb, the long steps were designed for donkeys. I thought, are you a donkey? But kept on walking, I felt a sudden fear go through me, in this narrow lane there is nowhere for me to go to protect myself. Is there a red dot on my back? I knew I had sweat on my forehead, but kept on walking. There were small doors in the walls every now and again. Then I could see an elderly man sitting on a stool outside one of them, he beckoned me to go in the door alongside him. I thanked him and went through the door, the old man followed me, I entered a large, beautifully furnished lounge, the old man showed me to a chair next to a table, I didn't hesitate, I scanned the wall for a window, but there wasn't any, could be concerned about that. An elderly lady appeared through a doorway with a mug of coffee and two sandwiches, she put them down on the table, put her hand up and said, 'You wait.'

I sipped the coffee, how did she know I like my coffee flat white with two sugars? But it was just what I needed, I enjoyed the sandwiches as well. I was very restless, so I got up and looked around the room, there were expensive paintings on the walls, an investment I suppose. I looked at the sideboard, there was a photo, quite old, of two girls, about 9 or 10 years of age, and a taller boy in-between them. I studied it longer, looking at the features of the girls and the young boy. There was another small picture, to me, it appeared to be drawn in charcoal, of a girl sitting next to a big black dog.

Then a gravelly voice startled me, it sent shivers up my back. 'Would you please sit down, Mr Harrison.' I sat down looking at him, keeping my face very stern. He sat down, he was dressed the same as before, but when he sat down his knees were slightly apart and he had a cane with a silver top across his legs. The bows on his shoelaces were tied up the opposite way, the top of his left eyelid was slightly down to the other, he had a small blemish on his left cheek, he was still wearing grey tight fitting gloves, but no nervous twitch with his thumb on the left hand.

'Well Mr Harrison, we have found the merchandise and are now in the process of purchasing these items, it will take more time. We will contact you in the near future, be patient. There is plenty to see in Rome.'

The big man seemed to appear out of nowhere and ushered me to the door. I went back outside into the lane. The big man pointed to the left to let me know which way to go, and the door closed.

I followed the lane, totally lost, then came to two lanes crossing each other, I mentally tossed a coin in my mind and took the right lane, and eventually came back to the main road, I took a cab back to my hotel, ordered a meal through room service and a double scotch and dry ginger.

I sat at the table trying to put things together in my mind. The Dude I just met seemed to be different. His personality didn't seem to be cold, the little things I could see were different, his shoelaces, the cane across the knee, the blemish on his cheek, the meeting at somebody's home, the pictures and the paintings. And the big man. It all ties up together, but does two and two add up to four?

Tiny, you've got to start thinking outside the box. My mind needs a rest and it's been a big day. Just then my food and drink arrived. I said thank you to the waiter and slipped him a tip. He smiled and said 'Gracias.'

I swallowed my scotch in three gulps, that was good, and it hit the right spot, I enjoyed my spaghetti Bolognese, being Italian, it was like heaven.

I looked again at my Masonic list. The Grand Lodge of Italy. I rang the secretary's number. A voice answered. 'Peter Walsh here.'

'Yes, my name is Ronald Harrison.' There was a chuckle at the other end of the line.

'Yes, Mr Harrison, may I call you Tiny.'

That took me a little by surprise. 'Yes, you may.'

'We have been expecting you, The Grand Lodge in Melbourne have informed us you will be here to give a small talk on Freemasonary in Australia.'

I blinked. 'Yes, if that is what you wish.'

'Well Tiny, your rank of Past Senior Grand Warden and Grand Sword Bearer. We have all your accreditation here. Our next Lodge meeting is being held tomorrow, I will have a car pick you up at 10.30 am, Full Regalia.'

'Yes, I will look forward to that.' I gave him the address of my hotel, and he said, 'You'll have to excuse me Tiny, my tea is ready, and if I don't go know, she will say Freemasonary again, and I believe you know what I mean, see you tomorrow.' We closed our phones.

I didn't sleep well that night, dreaming of the man I hit in the face, of the coldness of the Dude, the red spot on my chest, and I'm in a kill zone walking up an ally, and the meeting with the Dude again in somebodies private home.

I ordered a light breakfast, two eggs, three rashers of bacon, baked beans, two sausages, fried onions and mushrooms, and a tomato, three slices of toast and a flat white coffee! And I nearly forgot, Tiramisu cake for later.

Two hours later I dressed in my Masonic Regalia. I stood in front of the mirror, you don't look too bad me old son, I should impress somebody. My phone rang, it was Reception. 'There is a car waiting for you Sir.'

'I will be straight down.' A gentleman opened the car door for me, giving that handshake. 'Gracias.' I got into the car and was whisked away.

The Lodge was a very impressive building, which you would expect in Rome, they treated me with the upmost respect, I did my talk in the Lodge, and I got a standing ovation.

Later in the South, Peter asked me. 'What are you doing tomorrow Tiny?'

'Nothing at the moment.'

'Well, I'm doing a small tour of the Vatican tomorrow, would you like to join us?'

'Yes, I would.'

CHAPTER 12

Sunday morning Peter arrived to take me to the Vatican, we went to the left side of the Vatican, there were two Swiss guards to open the gate and let us in. Peter handed them his pass. And we were allowed to continue. I was very impressed with the size of the Vatican, everything was in marble, even chips of marble on the driveway. Peter drove up to a foyer, and I got out, so did Peter, another man parked the car. We went into a foyer, then into a reception room. Peter walked up to the reception desk. The man behind the desk nodded to Peter and said, 'Good Morning Sir, to Peter.' Peter replied 'Good Morning, Brother Joseph.'

Joseph said, 'Your four guests are waiting over there. There were four nuns waiting by the wall. Peter nodded to him, then walked over to the nuns.

'Good Morning, I am Peter Walsh and my colleague here is Mr Harrison, now I don't want you to be startled, but this man Mr Harrison is also from Australia, now I know one of you comes from Brisbane, one of the nuns nodded, and one of you comes from Sydney, another nun nodded, one of you comes from Melbourne, another yes, and the last nun said, 'And I come from Perth, we are here on a training course for the Holy Mother.

I wanted to lighten it up and said, 'Don't worry about me, I'm just an old bluey dog here for the ride.'

They all grinned.

Peter said, 'Now I'm going to take you to the most sacred spot in the Vatican, into the Scavi. The word Scavi means excavation, so please follow me, watch your heads, and be careful of the steps. He took us through a small archway, I had to duck my head, the steps we went down were very worn, we stopped in a narrow corridor. Peter said, 'These walls here, we do not know how old they are, so please do not put your hands on them, other walls have been put in to strengthen the foundations, now these small cubicles on your right, we believe they are Roman burial catechisms. I looked at the paintings on the walls, there were small jars on the shelves, they were definitely Roman. I was very impressed. 'Please let me know if you're having trouble.'

We went further down in single file, and it opened out slowly. There were iron bars surrounding a brick wall. Peter made sure everybody could hear him. 'Now this is the most sacred spot in the Vatican, you see that small arch in the brick wall, above it there are Roman letters it says. Here lies Peter. Yes, Peter, the disciple.' Peter continued. 'Some years ago a Pope wanted all of this cleaned out, it was full of rubbish washed in by rains and this is what they found, and they made it into a Chapel. It became too small, so the fathers to be put four large columns around it, and as you can see they also put a forty ton block of marble on top to create another chapel, soon this also became too small, so they repeated the process, now the pedestal in the Chapel stands on top of that. A visiting archaeologist asked if they found anything in the Scavi. The workers said they didn't know, then the archaeologist asked if there was anyone still living who might know. One man stepped forward. 'Yes there is, but he's a very old man now, he lives not far from here.' The archaeologist visited him, he was sitting outside his little home.

'Excuse me Sir, they tell me you were one of the people who cleaned the rubble from the Vatican Scavi.'

The man had trouble talking, and was very old. 'Yes I was, but it was many years ago.'

'Did you find anything unusual?'

'Yes, we did, you are the first person to ask me, wait here.' He went into his house, and came back with a box which looked very old. 'We found this box, and it's full of bones.' The old man looked at him with tears in his eyes. I have been guarding this sacred box for many years, and my time is nearly finished. Could you please replace them to their rightful place in the Vatican.'

The Archaeologist, with tears in his eyes, said, 'Yes, yes, it would be my greatest honour to do that for you. For you have been the guardian of the truth for many years.'He took them back to the Vatican, and initially they were denied, but they were of the right age to be Peter's bones, and after have forensic tests done, it was deemed that the bones of the man showed that he had eaten lots of fish because of the mercury in his bones, but the hands and feet were missing, this is because Peter was crucified upside down, and because his hands and feet were nailed to the cross his body fell off them. Now, if you'd like to follow me around the back of the tomb, they did this, so, you see on the right-hand side there is a small opening which in now highlighted by a light, you will see the bones of his feet. On your left there are the bones of his hands.' The four nuns were crying, and holding handkerchiefs to their mouths. I also had tears in mine, this was the truth, you could not deny. This was the evidence of the existence of Peter. Do I have words to express it? no. I just had to accept the truth.

Hour guide Peter said, 'If you'd like to follow me, I will take you to Peter's Chapel.' We came out into a stronger light, but still under the Vatican, he led us to a small Chapel, beautifully decorated inside, it took your breath away, there were small pews there, and an Altar at the far end. Peter said,

'Under the Altar lies Peters bones, the Pope has three in his private quarters, but when he is troubled, he comes down here to pray to Peter in private. Now Sisters, you will be taken up to the restaurant, when you have finished your meal, your further studies will continue. Tiny come with me.'

We went up a small staircase, and found we were in the Vatican. 'Tiny just walk and browse around, if anyone talks to you, tell them you're with me, then when you have finished return here.

I slowly walked around the Vatican trying to take it all in, past the statue of Mary holding Jesus. Looking at the statues of the disciples, I eventually came back to where I came in, and sat down on a marble stone. You can't take it all in, in just one day, you need to come back after your mind has had a rest, and I'm sure you'll see many things you didn't see the day before. I was a little bit startled as a white dove landed on the floor in front of me. It started pecking at the floor, as if it were looking for something. The dove turned around and faced me, it seemed to lift its shoulders, and put its head back slightly, and stared at me. For a minute we just sat there studying each other, then it took off in flight into the Vatican. An Elderly nun walked past me, and said, 'Our Mother Mary has blessed you, and will protect you.'

This was all getting too much for me to comprehend. The next thing I knew a man was standing alongside of me.

'Mr Harrison, I'm here to take you back to your hotel, if you would like to follow me.'

I walked into the foyer of the hotel, and the Receptionist said to me. 'Mr Harrison, there is an envelope here for you.' She handed it to me, I looked at it for a moment, thought to myself, you need a drink Tiny, and I went to the bar and ordered a drink.

Back in my room I opened the envelope, there was a plane ticket to Singapore, another ticket with a connecting flight from Singapore to Port Moresby PNG.

I sat there staring at them, yes, I could understand Singapore, that's on my way home, but Port Moresby PNG? Doesn't make sense. Who am I to wonder why, just to do, and bloody cry.

CHAPTER 13

MONDAY MORNING I was on a plane heading for Singapore in Business Class, there was plenty of room for my long legs. It was easy going through customs and immigration, they just ushered me through.

The lady sitting next to me was not the talkative type, and I enjoyed the time to myself, I thought about the Vatican, St. Peter's tomb, the white dove and the nun saying to me. The Lady Mary is with you, and protecting you.

We eventually landed in Singapore. I disembarked the plane. My connecting flight was not for another hour and a half, so I went down to the foyer to look at the gardens again and the ponds with the koi fish. I went to a cafe and ordered a flat white coffee and an egg and bacon roll. My mind went back to my dog, Jack, and my best friend, Joyce.

A gentleman, about in his 50s walked up to my table, he had long hair, but it was very tidy, he was wearing a grey suit and black tie, he was wearing a security badge around his neck; I looked up at him, and he said, 'Mr Harrison?'

I said, 'Yes.'

'May I sit down please?'

I replied, 'Yes,' and gestured him to the spare chair. His security pass didn't have either a photo or name on it, that I could see.

'May I call you Tiny?'

'Yes.'

'Tiny, I have been with you since Paris.' Then I remembered.

'You were the man behind me in Rome when I was talking to the gypsy girl.'

'Yes, I was given the task of protecting you, no matter what, you are my last assignment, I'm retiring, but I wanted to meet you face to face. I've never protected a man like you in my life.'

My mind went racing back to Paris. 'You were the man with the sniper's rifle and laser beam.' He nodded. 'And were you following me up the laneway?'

'Yes.'

'Then tell me, why the Dude met me in a private house.'

'Tiny you are a very modest man, you have one of the highest ranks in Freemasonary there is. You had a private tour of the Vatican, your credibility is outstanding,' he was just trying to tell you how much he respected you, and trusted you. 'You're one of the few men who can get through his armour. You are an old school police officer, very observant and methodical. They certainly picked the right man for this assignment. I have not told you this, or had this meeting with you. Now, when I was looking through the sights on my rifle you gave the Dude some documents which he went through very carefully, then he double checked them, looking for something, then he handed the back page to his colleague, who put it over a light, noted it to the Dude, who kept the documents.'

'Yes, I remember.'

'Keep that in your mind, you have got yourself involved in something far bigger than you could imagine, I don't know what it is. When they have finished with you, do not pursue it, step aside, and go home, and try to forget it ever happened.'

'Now, whoever you are, how did you get involved in this?'

'I was born into a little village high in the mountains, we never had any contact with the outside world, only in the market, where we sold sheep's wool, we were non-statistics, when I turned sixteen I was asked to join the army, back then you didn't have a choice. You would call it a Militia Force. I was trained in every aspect of self-defence, but I became a sniper, and was hired out to anybody who wanted my services. I have had no choice in the matter. I am a nobody, I don't exist, I don't have a birth certificate, and no passport which is mine, they are provided by those higher up. I am just like you, a pawn on the chess board. I am 50 years old, I've lived too long, and I must disappear as I know too much.'

He stood up, bowed his head to me and walked away!

CHAPTER 14

I BOARDED THE plane for Port Moresby, I was still a bit confused and more than a little frustrated, the plane was comfortable and I had plenty of legroom. I dozed off into a deep sleep.

The Flight Attendant woke me. 'Your meal Sir, and what would you like to drink?'

'A double scotch and dry ginger, one piece of ice please. I enjoyed the meal, it was very fruity. I was thinking back to the conversation I had with the man in the airport. The document over the lamp? What was on it? The tour around the Vatican. Saint Peters tomb, and the Dove, what did the old nun mean. And what the man said where he had come from, how he got into his lifestyle, which he had no control over. All very strange.

We eventually landed at Port Moresby; I disembarked and stood in the foyer looking for somebody who would be looking for me. I decided to go to the reception desk, a very attractive lady with olive skin asked me, 'May I help you, sir?'

'Yes, my name is Ronald Harrison, are there any messages for me?'

She looked at the papers to one side of her. 'Yes, Mr Harrison.' Has she read through the papers? 'Mr Harrison you're booked on a flight tomorrow morning at 6 am for New Caledonia. You'll be landing in Noumea, and are booked into the Airport hotel, everything has been arranged, your luggage will be on that flight.'

I thought for a moment, don't argue, just do it, I didn't need my suitcase.

'I will have somebody show you to the hotel.'

The next morning I boarded a small jet plane, all I knew about it, was that it was built by Boeing, that put my mind at ease.

A man sitting alongside me introduced himself. 'Good Morning, my name is Malcolm.' We shook hands.

'They call me Tiny, I'm on my long service leave.'

Malcolm replied. 'We have an office in Noumea, I visit it once every month, just to check the books. Have you been to Noumea before?'

'No, I haven't Malcolm.'

'Well, the French control it, and the minerals, between the Indigenous people and the French there is a very fine line, they tolerate each other, the French have the shops and other facilities. Club Med Hotel is on the far shore. My wife and I came here a few years ago on the Oriana, a cruise ship, there was another cruise ship in port that day called the Aleksandr Pushkin, both crews challenged themselves to a football match, this of course was nothing to do with the Captains, who both attended.

It was the roughest football match I've ever been to, it was declared a tie. My wife and I took a tour on a bus towards Club Med, the driver of the bus said 'on the left is the Aquarian Centre, on our right there is nude bathing, everybody on the left hand side of the bus got up and went to the right side, I thought the bus was going to tip over. When you order coffee make it very clear what you want, or you will get something completely different. The harbour has been split into two, with the tailing from the mines.'

We had a good smooth landing, and disembarked. A man walked up to me holding a sign. MR HARRISON.

'Yes, I am Mr Harrison.'

'Mr Harrison, I'm here to take you to the hotel, your luggage will be delivered direct to the hotel.'

I didn't argue, I didn't know the protocol here.

My suite was a little higher than the harbour, giving me a good view of the harbour and the yachts tied up at their moorings, and a long jetty.

The Receptionist told me there was a restaurant alongside the jetty. It was all very practical for visiting boats and yachts. In the far distance I could see a cruise ship and an oil tanker.

I went down to the restaurant, and lent on the handrail looking at the yachts. Another man came and lent on the handrail alongside of me.

He said, 'Very relaxing isn't it?'

I replied. 'Yes it is, two or three days here is what I really need, I have spent too many hours in the air.'

'My name is John.' I put my hand out and said, 'Tiny Harrison.'

'What brings you here Tiny?'

'I'm on my long service leave, I hope this is my last destination, from here I want to go home to Melbourne.' I could hear the emotion in my voice.

John said, 'Do you know anything about yachts Tiny?'

'Yes, and no, in my younger days I was coned into winding a coffee grinder on a racing yacht. I did about two years of that, then I joined the Police Force, and didn't have time for that anymore.'

'Then Tiny, you may be the man I am looking for. I was once the Top Manager of a shipping company, my time had come to retire, and I got involved in a Yacht Club, and my wife and I ended up buying that Schooner you see down there, she is called My Lady, we decided to sail to the Cook Islands, then slowly make our way back to Sydney. When we got here, my daughter rang my wife from Sydney, saying our youngest granddaughter was very sick in hospital, and asked her to come back home to help. I knew my wife had been away from the children for too long, and I didn't argue. So here is my problem, I need a sailing companion, at my age it isn't practical to sail a vessel like My Lady on your own.'

I looked at John for a few minutes, thinking, a way home to Australia, no-one has contacted me yet. Play the game, and see what happens.

'Tiny, can I buy you a drink and a meal.'

'John, I never turn down a free lunch.'

We found a table and ordered our drinks and meal.

'Well John, I have a few things to sort out, can I come back to you tomorrow.'

We drank, and talked until 11 pm. I liked this man, he was practical, straight and honest.

I woke to the sound of knocking on my door. I looked at my watch, 5 am, I put on my dressing gown, and carefully opened the door. I was surprised to see the Dude.

'Come in, come in,' he walked in slightly tapping his walking stick. I thought he's using the walking stick, it isn't for show. I pulled out one of the dining chairs, so that he could sit. He eased himself into the chair.

'I believe Tiny you have solved the problem of transport back to Australia. Yes Tiny, I was there, and I heard the conversation. Could you please arrange with John for my passage to Australia also.'

I thought, this is too easy Tiny, watch your step.

'I think John would like to meet with you first, before he made a commitment, and now would be the best time, as there won't be anyone around.'

The Dude looked at me very carefully, weighing the situation up in his mind. 'Yes Tiny.'

I put some clothes on and as we walked down to the jetty I noticed the Dude had a slight limp, we reached My Lady. I said to the Dude. 'She's a beautiful vessel, isn't she?'

The Dude just nodded.

'All the sails are on remote control, the galley has big windows and carpet, the stern is quite large with a heavy timber handrail around it.'

I took off my leather shoes, and climbed aboard, knocking on the roof of the galley. The hatch opened and out stepped John.

'Good morning Tiny.'

'Good morning John, this is Mr Dude, can we talk?'

'Yes, welcome aboard, come down into the galley.' The Dude was stubborn, and didn't accept any help to climb aboard, we sat down in the galley.

John asked. 'You both take coffee?'

I replied. 'Just a flat white for me, two sugars.'

The Dude, with his gravelly voice said, 'Same for me. John, we are both looking for passage to Sydney, and you are looking for travelling companions.'

John studied the Dude. 'I was the General Manager of a very substantial shipping company, I've never met you face to face, but we did do business together.'

The Dude said, 'Yes.'

John looked at him with piercing eyes, which I didn't like, but said, 'Welcome aboard, business wise I know you.'

The Dude's eyes narrowed. 'Then I will say the debit is paid.'

They both nodded to each other. John suggested the Dude would be better in the Master Suite forward, where he would have his own toilet, and shower, for your own safety, stay aboard. He looked out of the big windows to the jetty and surroundings.

'Nobody will know you're aboard.'

We finished our coffee, nobody said a word. Just then there was a slight bump on the deck. John said, 'How does she know whenever we're about to leave, she turns up, now I've got to buy more tins of sardines! 'we both looked up to see a big Pelican looking in the window. 'My wife found it all tangled up in fishing line, it was just about dead, she brought it back to life, and she's been with us all the time, when we get into port she leaves, when we're ready to sail, she's back.

John asked the Dude. 'Can you arrange for your luggage to be delivered? Tiny will you go and get yours, I'm going to buy more stores, and sardines, 2 bottles of brandy, and log my paperwork with the port authorities. Does anybody have any French money?'

I replied. 'Yes, I do, I'll get it when I get my luggage and I will meet you on the wharf.'

I started off to my hotel room, fetched my luggage and man bag. On the jetty I gave John the French money.

He said to me. 'The way of the world is the same all over, you want something, you have to pay.'

I went back to My Lady, the door to the Dude's cabin was closed, a van turned up on the jetty, on the side of it, it said Airport luggage. Two men got out, one had a clipboard, 'I've got five suitcases, one overnight bag, I scruffy suitcase for the vessel My Lady.' They put the five suitcases in the cabin very carefully, they were made of good quality leather, all identical, they dropped my suitcase on the stern.

The man with the clipboard said, 'Could you sign here.'

I hesitated, but didn't have a logical reason not to sign, so I did. He gave me the receipt, and they left. I took my suitcase down to one of the bunks, I decided to take the top one and put my Masonic case alongside the life jacket, and put my man bag on top of them.

I went back into the galley and made myself a cup of coffee, then I sat outside on the stern watching the other yachts, waiting for John to return, shortly a taxi arrived on the wharf, John got out and I went to help him with the stores, we returned to the boat and I made John a coffee. 'How did you go with the money John?'

'No problem, you have to pay for your paperwork, but there is a jar on the counter for you to give a donation for the widows of officers who have died in service to the ports. Do this and you don't have any trouble. There was a big luxury yacht here, they didn't give a donation to the widows, they received their papers a fortnight later! You don't mess with those in power. Tiny, could you slide those suitcases on to the bunks either side.' He pointed to them. 'They're underneath the cockpit, just pull those little cupboards open.' I did as he instructed, there were two little bunks, which were a little cramped to get into, but perfect for the suitcases.

John was filling out his logbook, when he had finished he turned to me saying. 'Tiny, I have to be totally honest with you, as you know I was looking for a sailing companion, I interviewed several, but none of them were suitable. A French government Politician came to see me, I knew him well. He said he'd been approached by the Australian government officials ASIO, he told me about you, and that he wanted to get you and another man to Sydney. He didn't give me the other mans' name. He said that he does not exist! And I thought I had left all the politics back in Australia, tip for tat, favour for favour, that's government politics, if I had known who the other passenger was, I would have refused, but a deal is a deal, make it and you can't back out. Tiny, 3 bacon and eggs, I'm starving. I'll pack away the stores and feed the Pelican.'

John finished putting the stores away, he then opened two cans of sardines, put a tablespoon of brandy into a glass and half filled it with water, then went out to the Pelican who opened his beak, and John emptied the two tins of sardines into his pouch, the Pelican lifted his head, and swallowed the sardines, John then emptied the glass of brandy and water into the Pelican's pouch, it swallowed it down, shook himself, then sat back on his legs, I would swear he was grinning.

John came back into the galley, picked up a plate of bacon and eggs and knocked on the door of the front cabin.

A voice said, 'What do you want?'

'Breakfast is served with coffee.' the door didn't quite open, just enough for a hand to come out and take the plate and coffee, then the door closed.

We ate our breakfast, I picked up the dishes and started to wash them up. John went to his chart table to fill out his logbook, he did a few calculations and said, '1000 km to Sydney, course southwest 240.' He started the motor. 'Tiny, let the power line and stern line go.'

I made sure the stern line did not foul the propeller. Noted this to John, and we were on our way, we were heading up the channel to the open ocean.

John said to me with a hesitant voice. 'We have company.' I looked to the stern. 'And there is a Coast Guard boat coming up on our starboard side about 50 to 60 metres from us.'

One man had a camera, he appeared to be filming us. The man at the helm saluted us, he gave me the sign of fidelity, I did the same back, then he gave me the hailing sign, was he telling me to be cautious? Nothing is as it seems. the Coast Guard vessel did a wide sweep to starboard and headed back to port.

'Tiny, that wasn't a camera, it was a heat seeking camera, they know there are three people on board, I only registered two. They look for stowaways on cargo ships.'

He started to laugh. 'Tiny, it was I who approached you in a restaurant, and you made the decision to sail with me. I said we will just wait, he who laughs last, laughs best.'

We didn't see the Dude for two days, he just put his hand out for food and drink. On the third day he appeared for his breakfast, and said to us.

'I really needed that rest, I hadn't really slept for a week.'

We finished our breakfast, and I got up to make coffee. John went up to make a sail change, the wind had shifted to another quarter, he came back down to the galley.

I said to the Dude. 'We are going to be aboard for the next couple of days, what I'm about to say, I will say it to nobody else, it stays on this vessel. When I first met you, you were sitting in a chair with a cane between your legs, your right hand was on top of the cane, your left thumb was stroking your index finger, I put it down to nerves, as you are doing now.' His thumb stopped rubbing his finger. 'Your shoe laces have been tied in a bow one way, because you are right-handed. Your ears are level with the rest of your features, I would say perfect symmetry.' That cold personality shone through his eyes. 'I met you again in Rome. You were sitting in a chair with your legs apart and your cane across your legs, your hips were a little bit wider, your shoe laces were tied up by a left-handed person. One of your ears was slightly below the other and you had a blemish on the left hand side of your cheek. You did not have a nervous twitch with your thumb. Your personality was warm, I would not say friendly, business is business, my observations of all the photos told me something where you had arranged this meeting. I now ask you to take that thing out of your mouth that changes your voice, it's annoying. You are one of a twin, the big man is your brother, and the reason you move from place to place so quickly is, your twin being your double. You are in one place and your twin is in the other.'

John was leaning up against the sink, he was fascinated. The Dude took the mouthpiece out of her mouth, and with a normal woman's voice.

'You are the old school Policeman, very observant, putting all the little pieces together, you don't deal with paperwork, you keep it simple. The moment you struck my brother-in-law in the nose so quickly, I knew you were professional, you are not an aristocrat, and you are very straight and wise, the same as John, you uncovered my facade which nobody else has done. I'm tired and worn out, and I believe I have met my equal, that's why they sent you. You are straight street wise, you will not bend your principles, honesty is number one with you. You proved that in Rome, with the high rank in Freemasonary, you do not get that easily. You had a private tour around the Vatican, your credentials are impeccable. I have never said this to anybody else. I am in your hands, or should I say your Governments' hands. I am not well, it is my time to disappear forever.'

John broke in. 'I think it's time for a drink,' he paused. 'Mr Dude, what do you drink?'

'A gin and tonic, thank you'

'A double scotch and dry for Tiny.' I nodded and looked the Dude straight in the eyes. Mr Dude, please do not put that mouth peace back in your mouth whilst on this vessel. She nodded.

John gave us our drinks, then he looked through the windows to make sure there were no other vessels close.

He startled us when he said, 'Oh, she is beautiful.'

We both stood up, we could see white clouds floating on the surface of the water, they were two, maybe three nautical miles to our starboard coming towards us. John reached into a shelf and took out a large pair of binoculars, he looked through them. 'It is the Daisy May, a high sided barque sailing clipper, a three master, she has all her sails set, she looks magnificent, with her white sails and blue hull, just gently riding the small swell, she is a Naval training vessel for future Captains in His Majesty's Navy. Winston Churchill brought her at the beginning of the war, she came under the Security Act. I would love to be her Captain.' John picked up the mic for his radio. 'My Lady to Daisy May, you bring tears to my eyes.'

A voice came straight back. 'My Lady, Captain Coe, your vessel looks extremely good as well. Our destination is New Zealand. Fair winds to you my friend.'

'Where did you get those binoculars John?'

They were already on this vessel Tiny when we bought her, they are the very best, made in Germany.

He sat down and asked the Dude 'How did you start off in life?'

There was silence for a few moments. 'I was born in a village high up in the mountains, we were not statistics to anybody, we didn't exist, we had our goats, our angora sheep and donkeys. My brothers and twin sister never wore shoes, we had a stream running through our village and we heated our water in a big tub, our food was whatever we could find in the mountains, I had a big dog, he was my best friend, one year we had a very bad winter, we were very short of food, my dog had become old and he was no different from the goats, sheep or donkeys, when they were no longer useful, their fur coats kept us warm in the winter. My father told me it was my dogs time to leave, he was no longer useful, and he became food on the table. My father used to take the angora wool to market once every two or three months, one day my sister and I went with him, he traded his wears in the market for salt, flour, pots and pans, knives and whatever had a practical use, no luxuries. But I could see others selling seeds, oils from plants that grew wild in the mountains, which we used for medicines, my sister and big brother collected these things from the mountain, ground them down, boiled them, then put them into leather bags or anything else we could put them in, and took them to the market. We were totally surprised when we were able to sell them for money, and my father was so pleased with us, that's how it started, and grew. Whatever we could sell we would do so for money, but we never traded human lives like others, who would sell their daughters and sons to the Militia to survive. I will say it again, to survive. In your world you have everything, doctors, hospitals, and governments give you money to survive, we live in two separate worlds, and you judge us, instead of judging yourselves. You live for pleasure, we live to survive. I have nowhere to go, nothing to do, so could I please have another gin and tonic.'

John didn't argue, he just gave her another drink.

'John, we did more work for you than you know. When you gave work to others in the shipping company abroad, they used to contact me, and I would solve their problems, but you would pay the piper well. Now I must rest.' The Dude picked up her glass, and went back to her forward cabin, and closed the sliding door.

John and I talked about what she had said, she didn't have a birth certificate, or a passport, to the world, she didn't exist, but she had created one of the biggest organisations in society. Where in our society she didn't really exist, for there isn't any paperwork to prove that she does. In a manner of speaking she lives in one world and we live in another…

The next morning the seas were moderately calm, and John had all My Ladies sails set, and we were moving through the water well, as I was cooking breakfast the Dude appeared, but as a woman, she was quite attractive, which surprised both of us, she had her hair down and wore a thin white blouse.

She nodded to both of us and said, 'I now feel comfortable and relaxed.'

She sat down and ate her breakfast, then sat back and sipped her coffee, the coldness in her had gone.

John suggested to her that she sit down in cockpit with the leather seats, she did so. John checked his figures and filled out his logbook, he went up to the stern while I did the dishes, and made 3 cups of coffee, I went up into the cockpit at the stern with the coffees, we all sat there quietly, just enjoying the tranquillity, the peacefulness and the gentle movement of the vessel, the gentle slip slap of water on the hull, it must have been an hour and a half before anybody said anything.

She then said, 'You two men are just what I need to put things into perspective, you cannot be used, as I have used men. Give a man power, give him a good hug, some toys, look after his sexual needs and you have him in the palm of your hand, he cannot survive without these items. He knows I can take it away anytime I wish. He must play my game. This is how I built my empire, I have made men, and I have destroyed men in big places. If you have played my game nobody else wants you. You are too dangerous, and you know too much, it is quite easy to dissolve a mans position when you own him. Have you used the same principles to climb the crazy ladder John?'

He looked at her with a scowl on his face. 'Yes, and no. There are some I have had to put in their place in the interest of the company, and in my interests in the Politics of running the company.'

She turned to me. 'Tiny, you were brought up on a farm the hard way, you drove trucks, you worked many hours that you were not paid for, but you felt this was your job, and your responsibility. You joined the Police Force, when the officer took your height with a sliding pole, he got 6 ft 51/2 inch, and said. That will do, 6 ft 6 inch. You worked your way up with hard men, especially on the docks, you became very street wise in your society, and you were made a Sergeant. But when the opportunity came to work in your country town, you took it, and were very highly respected for your high principles, could you survive in my world?'

'That's a very interesting question.'

We sat there, and didn't say a word for quite some time.

Then John said, 'Food Tiny, and I will get the drinks.'

I cooked steaks, mashed potatoes, peas, carrots and tomatoes, followed by ice-cream and peaches covered in strawberry topping. No complaints. After dinner I washed the dishes, John made coffee, and we continued our conversation.

John said, 'You never mentioned the women in your organisation?'

'Women from my village married men who worked for me, they did not need birth certificates. Marriages are performed in a different way to your world, and they are provided with high standards of living, and they kept their men happy. I pay them well. Men are no different in your world, or mine.'

She sipped her coffee, she seemed to be deep in thought, then she said, 'I don't want to leave, I want to stay here.' Tears started to flow, she said, 'I must rest now.' and she went back to her cabin.

We were both taken by surprise by her emotions.

The next day she came in for breakfast, she didn't mention yesterday at all. She then went out to the cockpit with her coffee, and sat there watching the sails, she ate her lunch and then returned to her cabin.

The next morning after breakfast John said, 'We are now officially in Australian waters.' and just before lunch he said, 'We have company, a quite large Australian customs vessel is approaching us.' He turned the vessel into the wind, and pulled down the sails. There was very little wind, and the seas were only moderate. The Coast Guard vessel pulled up alongside us, a man came aboard with an officer, I recognised the man, he was from ASIO, I had met him in Melbourne.

'Good Morning Mr Harrison, it's very good to see you again.'

I didn't reply, I just stared at him. Then said, 'Get it over with.'

John said, 'What you want is below.' the officer put his hand into the air. Two cadets came aboard, and John went into the galley with them, they came back with the five suitcases. The man from ASIO said, 'You have another piece of merchandise which is very valuable.' The Dude appeared in the hatchway, and said to the ASIO man in a very cold manner. 'Get my suitcase, and my bag.' The officer went below and came back with her bags. With her gravelly voice she said to John. 'It has been a great honour to be aboard this vessel with you.' Then she turned to me. 'Tiny, I should have met you 45 years ago, but you live in one world, and I live in another, thank you for your companionship, we will not meet again, which makes me very sad.' She turned and left with the man from ASIO.

I watched them board the Coast Guard vessel and transfer to the helicopter which was on board, it took off and was gone, along with the Dude.

The officer said to me. 'There is another helicopter coming for you.' He turned to John, 'We have a replacement for you. You registered two on board, you must arrive back in Sydney with two on board.' Just then a female cadet came aboard, she had a clipboard, and was wearing shorts and a tight fitting shirt.

I said to John 'I told you I would have the last laugh, what are you going to tell your wife when she sees this lady aboard?'

John looked at me with a concerned look. I gave a little chuckle.

Just then a tall man climbed on board, his hair was much like mine, and about my build, he had a rucksack with him. John said, 'Thank God for him.'

The officer said, 'This is Malcolm Fraser, he will be your shipmate.'

John put his hand out saying. 'I am John.' He looked at me, and said to Malcolm. 'It's a pleasure having you aboard. You can have the bunk on the Port side.'

Another helicopter arrived onto the Coast Guards boat. The officer said to me. 'That's your helicopter, the young cadet had my suitcase, my Masonic case and my man bag. She looked at me saying 'I have put your wash items into the case.'

I could only say Thank you. I turned to John, put out my hand and shook his. 'We will meet again John, I've enjoyed our voyage, thank you.'

I turned and climbed aboard the Coast Guard vessel and transferred to the helicopter, next thing I knew we were in the air heading for land, and I was looking down at My Lady, I thought to myself, thank you.

CHAPTER 15

We landed at a Military base, and I was ushered to another aircraft. I sat down in a seat with plenty of leg room. Two or three men board the aircraft wearing military uniforms. Then a lady boarded, she reminded me of Penny Wong, but it wasn't her. She looked down at me. 'May I sit down with you Tiny?'

I hesitated, how did she know my name, she obviously was a lady of influence and connections.

'Yes, please do.'

'My name is Pananda.' The seat belt sign went on, and we were in the air. I could feel the pressure in my stomach from the quick take off.

Pananda smiled. 'Yes, it takes a little getting used to.'

I started to undo my seat belt, but she said to me. 'No Tiny, leave it on, you are on a special military flight, this is a special jet and it flies at a very high speed.'

We sat there getting comfortable. 'Tiny, I work for the government in Canberra, you have just finished an assignment, and it has been very successful, you are being flown back to England where you started, you will attend a large meeting to prove you are there. We must cover your tracks. When you left Rome the five items left with you as your luggage. The man in question always works that way, as you know, he doesn't exist, as you are a Government official, you signed for them on behalf of the Australian Government. The man in question has terminal cancer. And because of his situation in society we made an agreement with him. We would give him the best medical attention we could, he is now in a military hospital which overlooks the sea. We agreed that when he dies you would take his ashes back to Rome, so they can be scattered where he was born. He said that you would know where to take them. So we would say you're going back to Rome with your companion Joyce. We will foot all the bills, and we won't interfere.' She chuckled. 'You cannot refuse, we went to a higher authority, The Grand Master.'

I looked at her for a moment, then said, 'Shifty, very shifty.'

She looked at me seriously. 'Mr Ronald Harrison, you are a special man, now I think we both need a drink, and something to eat.'

She raised her hand and a flight attendant appeared, she ordered, she knew exactly what I wanted. We ate our meal and finished our drinks.

'Tiny, would you excuse me, I have to run over some paperwork with my colleague for our next meeting. I've been most honoured to meet you and hope we will meet again.' She stood up, looked at me with a very warm smile. 'Good bye Tiny.' Then she went and sat down next to another man, who handed her some paperwork. I sat back and made myself comfortable and closed my eyes.

The next thing I knew we were landing in a military airport. The flight attendant said 'We are changing pilots and refuelling before take off for London.'

The lady I was talking to, disembarked saying 'Good Bye'. I nodded.

We eventually reached our destination. London. I was taken back to the guest house I stayed in before. The Receptionist said, 'Good Morning Tiny, can I order you some breakfast, bacon, eggs, two pieces of toast, onions and sausage.'

I sat in the dining room, ate my breakfast and drank my coffee, I was feeling a bit weary, jet lag again, but this jet lag was a bit heavier, I picked up my keys from Reception.

'Jarrett, were are my two cases?'

He winked at me and looked at me seriously 'They are in your room Tiny, where they have been all the time.'

I was too tired to play games, went up to my room, showered and went to bed. I woke up at 5 am trying to clear my head, I made myself a strong cup of coffee, sipping it quietly, trying to get everything together in my mind. So I was right, the Dude was not well, we had given her the way out. How can I judge her, what do I think of her. Would I say it is very confusing, do I like her? Yes, but No. She always said. To survive anything, to survive. She had spoke of her dog and what her father said to her to survive. Hard and Cruel, but it was the practical truth in her world.

There was a knock at the door, I opened it, and there was a man I had first met in England, Terry Barker, he had two other men with him.

'Did you get our message Tiny.'

'No, I didn't.'

'Well, we're off to Torbay in Devon today for lunch. You get ready.'

I didn't argue, I had been warned.

Driving down through the English countryside in the front seat of a very comfortable vehicle was what I needed to take my mind of all the events that had happened.

The ring road around London was very practical, we went down to Devon via Bristol.

Terry pointed to the big bridge saying. 'That is the way to Wales, we're very proud of that bridge.'

The tide was out in the Bristol channel, there were plenty of mud banks. Further down the motorway I was fascinated with the amount of wind turbines. Australia should have a good look at these, progress.

We eventually went through Exeter on to Torbay, and arrived at the Masonic Lodge. It was very old, the front entrance was very impressive. The Master of the Lodge introduced himself. 'I am Mike Doolan, the Master of the Lodge at the moment, but somebody is ready to knock me off my perch. We had a visitor from Australia a few years ago, his name was Trevor Evans, have you ever met him?'

'No, I don't think so.'

'He was a very interesting character, I'm quite sure you would have liked him. Now, let me show you around before Lodge starts.'

We went into the South. I was very impressed by the amount of portraits of past Freemasons hanging on the walls, the big board with all the past Masters names, they went a long way back, then we went into the Lodge room, it took my breath away, it was like walking into the Vatican, Majestic paintings around the walls of Freemasons performing the rituals, if a word slipped your mind, it was there in the paintings. But if you're not a Freemason, and had not passed through the rituals, you wouldn't understand. I was very impressed. We were offered coffee and sandwiches. The ceremony started, and I was introduced into the Lodge.

When the ceremony finished in Peace and Harmony, we went into the South for refreshments. I gave my talk about friendship and the connection between brothers around the world. I got a standing ovation. Mike Doolan thanked me for the talk, others shook my hand. Terry said 'We had better make a mile, it's a long way home.'

The next thing I knew I was walking into the foyer of the Bed and Breakfast. Jarrett said to me. 'Your plane ticket has come through to my computer. Flight back to Australia at 2.30 pm.' He handed me the paperwork.

'Thank you Jarrett.'

'Anytime Tiny.'

The next morning I went down for breakfast, the waiter said, 'The usual Tiny?'

'Yes please.'

A couple sitting further down had a dog with them, he looked just like my Jack. I felt a bit emotional. That could be Joyce and myself with Jack.

A voice startled me, and I looked up, the two men I had met before in this restaurant when I first arrived, were standing there.

'May we please join you Tiny?'

I gestured with my hand for them to sit down. 'You apparently did a remarkable job Tiny, credit must be given.'

I thought that's a bit arrogant.

'Now Tiny, you have something of ours, and we have something of yours.' He put his hand under the table and showed me my watch, I took off the watch I was wearing, and we swapped. 'Now Tiny, you never changed the time on this watch?'

'No, I didn't want to freak things up. I just sorted out the correct time in my mind.'

'Now the serious part Tiny, we lost track of you when you went into the Vatican, but we do know the Vatican has its own electronic locking equipment. The next day you went to the Vatican and then went for a walk. The tracking device in the watch stopped working, why, we don't know, please tell me where you went.'

My mind went back to the plane, in the conversation with Pananda, she had said that the Dude had trust in me. No my principles had been pushed to the very brink, and I will say to the breaking point, don't push them any further.

The other man said, 'We can hold you in England until you give us what we want.'

'I am employed by the Australian government, I have been on their business, I don't think you would like a political incident would you.? When I first joined the government department,

I swore an oath to Australia, not to the Commonwealth, have I made myself clear gentlemen?'

Neither of them answered, then the first man said, 'Now the expenses we gave you, do you have any left?'

'No, I don't.'

The man just nodded, and rubbed his hands together. 'I think we will have some breakfast.' They both ordered breakfast and coffee.

When their meals arrived I said to the waiter. 'Their breakfast does not go down to my room, they pay for their own.'

One of the men raised his eyebrows and said to the other. 'They told us not to play games with Tiny Harrison.'

'Now gentlemen, if you would please excuse me, I have a bag to pack and paperwork to do.'

I left them sitting there. A little shiver went up my spine. I did swear to Her Majesty the Queen and the Crown.

I boarded the aircraft for Melbourne, Business Class, I was given the same seat as I had before. A man came and sat down beside me, we introduced ourselves.

He said to me. 'Thank goodness I don't have to walk around anymore, my stump is bloody sore.'

I didn't know what he meant until he pulled his jeans up on his right leg, then twisted his leg, I didn't believe what I was seeing, his leg slid forward and his foot went to one side, then I realised he had an artificial leg. He said to me. 'They always put me here, it's easier for them to throw me out if there's a problem.'

CHAPTER 16

24 HOURS LATER we arrived back in Melbourne, Chris O'Hara, my 2IC picked me up from Melbourne Airport, being his normal, tactful, friendly person. He said to me. 'You look bloody terrible, you need another holiday.'

'It's good to see you again Chris. Now take me home, I will go to sleep so I won't see you driving.'

I was so surprised we found it back onto the freeway, we needed to stop for fuel. Chris said, 'Have you got any money for fuel?'

I thought, he hasn't changed one bit, it's just how I left. I gave him a $50 note, he went to pay and came back with two cups of coffee and two egg and bacon rolls. I thought to myself, damn jet lag, this is a Police vehicle, he would have paid with his Police credit card, he put the two coffees in the coffee holders. And gave me my roll, I sat there staring at him.

He said, 'What's wrong?'

'There wouldn't be any change by chance?'

'Well Tiny, there is fuel, coffee, and egg and bacon rolls.'

'Chris, this wouldn't by any chance be a Police vehicle?'

He very reluctantly gave me the change. I just shook my head and said, 'Thank you.'

He took me straight home, I could hear Jack barking in the house, when I opened the door he nearly knocked me over, I kept rubbing, stoking and cuddling him. 'I have missed you Jack.'

Then I heard Joyce's voice. 'Well, look what the cat dragged in Jack, he hasn't rung us once to let us know where he is, or how he is, now give me a cuddle, then I will make you a cup of coffee.'

Joyce made the coffee and gave me my cup. 'Tiny where have you been, you have lost weight and you don't look yourself.'

I couldn't stop the tears; I just sat there sobbing; it had finally all caught up with me. I was home; I was safe; I was no longer playing the game. Jack and Joyce are now with me. 'Joyce, I just need to sleep; it has been a long journey.'

She didn't argue, she just helped me to bed. Jack laid alongside me, and I fell into a deep sleep.

The next morning Joyce was there with a cup of coffee. 'Tiny it's 11 am. You have slept around the clock.' She handed me my mobile phone. 'Tiny, the children have been worried, ring them.'

The next morning I was back in the Police Station, sitting at my desk. I had left everything neat and tidy. Now there is paperwork all over the desk. I felt a little annoyed. Then thought, they have missed you Tiny, how else could they show me, I am back where I belong.

Frank came into my office with two cups of coffee, and sat down in a chair. 'Good to see you back Boss, did you have a good holiday?'

'Yes Frank, did everything and went everywhere.'

'Just after you left Tiny, Trevor passed away, but he was happy you had put his son in the right place. George Sharmon paid his fare back to Melbourne, and his return flight. We all attended the funeral, and the Commissioner was there, he gave a small talk and put in your apology.'

'That was good of him Frank.'

Frank didn't say anything for a moment, he just sipped his coffee. 'Tiny, you remember that young lady you arranged accommodation for.'

'Yes Frank.'

'Well I visited her from time to time, in my own time, not on Police time. We talked a lot, we seemed to get the same thoughts and ideas. Well, I took her out to dinner with the children, on the way home we stopped at the children's park, and I played with the children. When we got back to her house, and had coffee, she took me by surprise when she asked. 'Will you Marry me?' I didn't hesitate, I said Yes. After a few tender moments she asked me when would you be back, I said that I didn't know. She asked me 'Do you think Tiny would give me away at our Wedding?'

'Sorry Boss, but I said Yes.'

'Frank, what are you sorry about, when my back was turned, you got the girl. Do you think I would have to wear my dinner suit?'

'Tiny, I will leave that for the Bride, it is her day.'

Everything settled back down. Life continued as normal. About ten weeks later the desk told me that the Commissioner of Police is on his way today. I leaned back in my chair and shouted out. 'Chris, you've got problems. The Commissioner of Police will be here shortly.' like an old mother hen flapping her wings around, he started flapping around. 'Have you finished your morning tea? Then get four cars out on the road, and only return when we call you, or if you have somebody to arrest, and bring them back here, the cells are empty.' To another Policeman he said, 'Clean up the lunchroom, tidy everything up.'

I thought, he is The Commissioner of Police, not God, and he's not a fool.

About an hour later the Commissioner arrived with another man whom I recognised straight away. He was carrying an overnight bag and a smaller one, he put them on my desk. I looked at the small one, a cold shiver went up my spine, I knew what it was. The Dude is now free. I knew the Commissioner was talking to me, but I couldn't take my mind off the small case, was it all just a dream? The Dude, he is no more, the Dude never existed. But I had met the Dude, I turned to the Commissioner. 'Excuse me Sir, I didn't hear what you were saying.'

'I said Good Morning Tiny, I have another task for you to do.' The Commissioner corrected himself. 'No, no. The Prime Minister has another task for you to do, and now you outrank me.' He slid a small box over to me, I hesitantly opened it, inside was a medal and a handwritten note, it said. Ronald Harrison (Tiny), with my deepest respect I install upon you this rank, unfortunately I cannot officially present this to you under the protocol of the Secrecy Act. On behalf of Australia, and its Government. Thank you.

I stared at the medal. Yes, there were tears in my eyes, not for the medal, but for the Dude. I closed the lid, and put the box in my man bag.

'The Prime Minister requests that you deliver this small case to the Dude's family. The Prime Minister said you knew where they were.'

Another little shiver went through me, remembering that laneway. The Commissioner handed me an envelope. 'Inside this envelope there are two return tickets to Rome, one is for you, the other is for Joyce. Both of you will be on holiday for ten days, there are expenses in the envelope. We did not supply you with these! Now, the other overnight bag is a present for Joyce. I hope my wife Chris never sees it, she'll want one, and I certainly couldn't afford it on my salary.'

I looked at how beautifully it had been made, the stitching was definitely hand done, it was all handmade.

'Can I buy you a cup of coffee? I noticed a coffee shop just down the road, and we can sit outside under a tree.'

I called out to Chris O'Hara, and before I could blink, he was there by my side.

'Commissioner, may I present my 2IC Chris O'Hara. Chris this is the Commissioner of Police Peter Smith.' They shook hands.

'The Commissioner and I are going down for a coffee, these two bags contain gold, I leave them in your care, you can sit in my chair.

We went down to the coffee shop and the Commissioner ordered two coffees, we sat under the tree. 'Tiny, tell me about the Dude, you are the only one of a few who have actually met him.

I thought for a few moments. 'The Dude was born in the mountains, in a different world to us, no birth certificates, no passports, a non statistic. The Dude was highly intelligent, and very streetwise, he found his own way to survive in his world not in ours. The Dude became one of the most successful business people in his world. Like Kerry Packer in our world. You want something, and are prepared to pay, they will find it for you. I have the deepest respect for the Dude. The Dude would say, it's all about survival. In respect to the Dude, that's all I will say.'

'Thank you Tiny. A few words with a lot of meaning. Well Tiny, time ticks on, and I have another meeting to go to. Have a relaxing holiday.'

CHAPTER 17

I WENT HOME and put the two bags on the table, then gave Jack some attention. 'Yes, yes Jack, I'll get your dinner.'

I gave him his dinner, turned around and there was cat up on the table sniffing around the bags. 'Cat, you are nosy, come on and I'll feed you.'

I fed cat, and got myself a drink, sat down in my arm chair, and looked at the small case. Memories came flooding back through my mind, but the best one was a lady sitting in the cockpit of the sailing boat, looking very relaxed and peaceful.

Just then Jack started to bark, by his reaction, I knew it was Joyce. She made a fuss of him, then she walked over and kissed me on the forehead.

I said to her. 'The overnight bag on the table is yours.'

She looked at it, then said, 'Oh, it's lovely, where did it come from?'

I hesitated, then said, 'A friend of mine in Rome.'

She turned around with a puzzled look on her face. I had to block anymore conversation. 'Have a look inside Joyce.'

She was just as impossible as me. Joyce ran a hand over the leather. 'This is beautiful.' She slowly undid the zip and opened it. I walked over to have a look, but Joyce put up her hand. 'No, no, it's my present, wait.' Then she said in a puzzled voice 'Dom Perignon France.' She took out a bottle, and just looked at it. 'Tiny, this is very expensive wine, and there are four bottles. Do we open one now?'

I grinned. 'Why don't you wait until after our holiday?'

'What holiday?'

'Well, I have two tickets for Rome, but if you don't want to go, I could take Jack.'

'Tiny, could you give me a minute to think about what you just said. Do I like Rome? I've never been to Rome, it's a long way away, what do I wear. I will go home early tomorrow, and pack my suitcase.'

Joyce opened one of the bottles of Dom Perignon, and poured out two glasses, I sat back in my chair, Jack sat in his $600 armchair, Joyce sat in her chair, I put the news on, I like the weather forecast the most. Joyce had just started to doze off, Trump had just finished talking, and a reporter said, 'The Government has just attained five parts of chemicals to protect Australia from chemical warfare, now we'll go to the weather report over Victoria. I sat up straight in my chair, are they saying chemical warfare?

Joyce lifted her head. 'What did you say Tiny?'

'Would you like some more wine Joyce?'

'Yes please.'

I held the bottle and two glasses, but I was looking at the other bag on the table, I shook my head, I am just a pawn in the game.

The next morning at breakfast I opened the envelope the Commissioner had given me, there were two tickets for a return flight to Rome.

Our flight is at 6 am tomorrow! We arrived at the airport, by the time we had parked the car it was 5.15 am, we checked in our luggage. I had my man bag, and the small bag, Joyce had her new overnight bag.

She said, 'I look like somebody special.'

I replied. 'You are somebody special Joyce.'

The flight to Rome was in Business Class, and was most comfortable. If Jack could see these armchairs, he would want one.

We disembarked, and went through Customs.

The Customs Officer asked me. 'What is in the small bag Sir?'

I replied. 'A good friend of mine's ashes. He wants to be buried where he was born.'

The Customs Officer stared at it for a moment, then looked at my passport again, stamped it, and said, 'Good Morning Sir.'

Joyce practically walked straight through, she nudged me with her shoulder. 'They know I'm perfectly innocent, just by my overnight bag.'

We went straight to the hotel, the same one I stopped at before. 'Would you like to go out and have some tea Joyce?'

'No thank you Tiny, I just want to sleep.'

'First thing in the morning Joyce, I will deliver this bag. If I'm not here, that's where I shall be.

The next morning I awoke at 6 am, showered, and got dressed, made a cup of coffee, I was sipping it thinking about the winding lanes and the names I couldn't pronounce, I was surprised how vividly it had come back to me. I rinsed out the cup, picked up my man bag and the other bag. I looked at it for a moment, the appearance of the bag wasn't a good look to walk down the streets. Joyce had one of those carry bags she had bought in the airport to say she was in Rome. I put it in that bag and left for my destination. I got a taxi to the Vatican. I stood there for a few moments to get my bearings. Now, I know where I'm going. I noticed a man leaning up against a wall, he puzzled me, once a Policeman, always a Policeman, he was reading a newspaper upside down, he was standing with one foot on the other, you would have thought he wanted to pee. I noticed a small round hole in the newspaper. He started to follow me, I turned up the 1st lane, then stood in a shadow. He appeared.

I stepped out. 'Is there something you want?' He stopped abruptly, looking for a way out, but I had blocked that. 'Now that camera you have must be very expensive, how many pieces do you think it would break into if I smashed it up against the wall?'

'A man has to make a living, I sell the photos to anybody who wants to buy them. I noticed the Australian accent.'

I took my badge out of my inside pocket, and showed it to him. 'I am Sergeant Harrison, and I'm on holiday, if I was not on holiday, I would want your name and your address, and charge you with the Privacy Act, now go away and let me enjoy my holiday.'

He turned and left, I thought to myself, did somebody employ him to follow me?' I found the small alleyway I wanted, and ducked my head to enter. I took a couple of steps into the alleyway, and leant against the wall waiting for somebody else to enter, when I realised there wasn't anybody following me, I continued on my way.

I found the doorway with a small stall outside, and knocked on the door. There wasn't any answer, but I heard a sound above me. I looked up, another sound, like a small window closing, but I couldn't see it. Then the door opened, and the old lady who was there before had the door opened for me, she looked at me, then to the bag I was carrying, she ushered me in, and I went down the steps into the lounge, first thing I noticed was all the paintings were gone, and quite a bit of the furniture, the old man was sitting in the far corner staring at me. The big man came into the room, stopped, and stared at me. I took out the other bag, and handed it to him, he took it by the handles, then put both arms around it, and started to sob, a loud noise came out of this throat, emotional grief, and put his head down on the box, and just cried, his big chest heaved up and down. His sister came out of the door, she was about 45, very attractive with long hair, my mind went back to My Lady and her twin sister. She looked at her brother who was now sitting in a chair, she put her arms around his neck, and started to cry. The old lady went over to her husband and held his hand. The big man stood up and gave his sister the box, she sat down on the couch and put her arms around the box, rocking back and forwards, crying.

The big man said in a soft voice. 'Thank you for bringing our sister home, she said you were her friend, you were there when she needed a friend, you understood the circumstances to her life, and what made her in our world, she could not have friends. To trust somebody in our world is dangerous, she said when she met you, that you are everything she ever wanted, you are straight down the line, your principles are impeccable, you will not bend. You will not let anybody have your soul. Your ethics are beyond reproach, shake your hand, and it is a binding contract.'

The elderly lady brought me coffee, and I sat down at the table. The big man said the Dude is now gone, and we will return to where we came from. Just disappear. The world of electronics is moving in, and we cannot compete.'

I said to them. 'I have a colleague with me, I told her I would be back by mid-day, so I must leave you, you have all taught me a lot about the other world you live in.'

I stood up, and put my hand out and shook his.

The old lady said, 'How do we pay you?'

'You already have, you have protected Australia from the most terrible thing that could happen, but now we are prepared.'

She put her arms around me, and kissed me on the forehead. 'Good bye Tiny Harrison.'

I picked up the empty bag, before I could leave she put a beautiful angora jumper in the bag.

I said, 'Thank you.' and left.

When I got back to the hotel Joyce was tidying up the room, I started to say staff will do that, but changed my mind, Joyce is Joyce.

I gave her the bag, and she took out the jumper, and held it in front of herself. 'Oh Tiny, it is beautiful, where did you get it from?'

'Some friends of mine who make them. Where would you like to go this afternoon Joyce?'

'The Vatican Tiny'

And we were off on our holiday, we got back at 8 pm and had a good meal.

Joyce said, 'All I want to do now is sleep, and get rid of this jet lag.'

The following day we went to the Parthenon, in the afternoon we went to the Trevi Fountain and watched people throwing coins in for good luck, we ate at a small restaurant, Joyce had Pasta, and I had a steak, Joyce said it was the best Pasta she ever had.

The next day we went to the Tivoli Gardens, 30 km outside of Rome, we took a bus tour, we saw the Villa d'Este, a 16th Century Villa which was built on a hillside, and is famous for its dramatic terraces and hundreds of gravity-powered fountains.

W had lunch at a hotel, when you went down the marble steps to the toilets the floor was made of glass 5 inches thick, through the glass you could see the ruins from hundreds of years ago, it was left exactly how they found it.

On the 4th day we were tired and had a sleep in, we had lunch in the hotel. And sat outside on the pavement sipping coffee. A young gypsy girl walked over to our table, she was carrying a tray with a strap around her shoulders to support it.

I said to her. 'I met you before, didn't I?'

She nodded, I looked at the trays, they were handmade bangles, made of copper wire, intertwined in the wires were small stones, they were beautifully entwined. Joyce picked up one and put it on her wrist. 'I like this one, it is plain and simple, and the stones are from Rome, she picked up one of the necklaces and stared at it, one big stone and three other smaller stones either side of it. Joyce said, 'The seven hills of Rome, they're also beautifully entwined in the copper wire, Joyce put in around her neck. I took out $40 from my expense money, and gave it to the young girl, she nodded to say yes, then she picked up another bracelet and gave it to Joyce, I gave the young girl the money, and put my hand in my pocket and took out the stone she had given me before. I pointed to the spare chair and she sat down. I waved to the waiter, he came over to us.

'Could I have another flat white coffee, two sugars for the young lady please.

The waiter said, 'Excuse me Sir, but we do not serve the gypsy's.'

I felt angry, and in my best Police voice is said, 'The young lady is just trying to survive, my colleague Joyce is a secretary and is also just trying to survive, you are a waiter trying to survive, I am a Police Sergeant, trying to survive. Now get me another white coffee, two sugars for the young lady, thank you.'

He returned with a white coffee and put it down in front of the young lady and left.

Another man came out wearing a white apron and looked at us, I put my hand in my inside pocket and took out my Police badge and put it on the table. The man looked at us, shook his head and left.

The next four days we booked various bus tours to Roman buildings, wineries and olive groves, we sat, talked and drank coffee and beautiful wines.

Our holiday had come to an end, it was now our time to go home. We boarded our flight home to Australia, sat back in our Business Class seats, a little exhausted, but totally relaxed. The plane took off, and we were served wine and light refreshments.

Joyce cuddled into my arm. 'I've so much enjoyed this holiday, you have been all mine, we have done so much together in such a little time, no matter what happens in the future, I will cherish these memories.' and she fell asleep.

My mind took over, the little gypsy girl had taken my suggestion, would she make another Dude in her world? I wonder, I hope so. Then I dozed off to sleep.

Our flight attendant gently woke us, and food was served.

Joyce said 'I keep on forgetting to give you this envelope, I found it in the bottom of the overnight bag.'

I opened it and read it. 'Joyce, I know you will take good care of Tiny, he is a very special man, in the world we live in today. They are very rare. He has high principles and ethics, he is straight down the line, and will not let anyone else use his soul, he thinks about the yes or no, or the left or right very carefully. I am very proud to say he was my friend. Yours sincerely the Dude.

One could say this is the end. But another would say this is just the beginning to another's survival.

I once asked a man if he would take a position for me, he said Yes, with no hesitation.

I have taken his ethics, his principles and his morals and his dedication to duty.

I have created a fictional story from this man's personality, he has been given a task by his country to find something for them to protect Australia, and because of whom this man is, he has achieved it.

If I have offended anyone, I apologise.

www.ingramcontent.com/pod-product-compliance
Lightning Source LLC
Chambersburg PA
CBHW061538050726
47593CB00002B/820